The Joyful Revolution

Anshumala Singh

Published by Anshumala Singh, 2024.

This is a work of fiction. Similarities to real people, places, or events are entirely coincidental.

THE JOYFUL REVOLUTION

First edition. October 8, 2024.

Copyright © 2024 Anshumala Singh.

ISBN: 979-8227907585

Written by Anshumala Singh.

The Joyful Revolution

Dear Reader,

Welcome to *The Joyful Revolution: How Two Oldies Plan to Save the World!* I'm thrilled to have you here as we embark on this heartwarming adventure with Martha and George—two unlikely heroes with a simple mission: to spread happiness, one small act at a time.

This story was inspired by the idea that the world could always use a little more joy, and that sometimes the most unexpected people, in the most unexpected ways, are the ones who bring it. In a time when we often find ourselves caught up in the hustle and bustle of life, it's easy to forget the power of connection, kindness, and laughter. Martha and George are here to remind us that even the smallest gestures—like a smile, a kind word, or a shared laugh—can make a big difference.

As you read this story, my hope is that it will bring you not only moments of joy but also a sense of how easy it is to brighten someone else's day. You'll join Martha and George as they fumble through pranks, organize spontaneous picnics, and discover that sometimes, the simplest things are the most powerful.

Their journey is a reminder that happiness isn't always found in grand gestures or big achievements. It's in the little things—whether it's sharing a cup of tea with a neighbor, planting flowers for a stranger, or just being present for someone who needs a friend. Martha and George show us that no matter our age or circumstances, we all have the ability to create joy, both for ourselves and for others.

So, as you dive into this story, I invite you to think about the small ways you can spread a bit of happiness in your own life. After all, the Joyful Revolution isn't just about two old friends—it's about all of us.

Thank you for joining this revolution of joy. I hope you enjoy the journey as much as I've enjoyed writing it!

With excitement and joy,

Anshumala Singh

Preface

The idea behind *The Joyful Revolution: How Two Oldies Plan to Save the World* was born from a simple question: *What would happen if two ordinary people, armed with nothing but kindness and a few quirky ideas, set out to make the world a happier place?* In a world that often feels divided and chaotic, this story aims to remind us of the importance of connection, laughter, and the joy that comes from the smallest acts of kindness.

This book is a lighthearted exploration of friendship, resilience, and the idea that no matter our age or circumstances, we all have the power to spread happiness. Through the antics of Martha and George, you'll see how a simple smile, a kind note, or a shared moment can have a ripple effect, touching lives in unexpected ways.

As you read, my hope is that you'll find moments that make you smile, laugh, and reflect on the power of small actions. You'll discover that even in the face of setbacks, laughter and kindness can be the best solutions. Martha and George's journey shows that making the world a better place doesn't require grand gestures—it just takes a little heart and a willingness to try.

This is not just their revolution; it's ours. Together, we can all make a difference, one small step at a time.

Introduction

In a small town where people have fallen into the rhythm of busy, disconnected lives, something unexpected is about to happen. Martha and George, two elderly friends who many would consider "past their prime," decide that their town—and maybe even the world—needs a bit more joy.

Armed with sticky notes, rubber ducks, and plenty of mischievous ideas, they embark on what they call "The Joyful Revolution." What begins as a few small pranks and spontaneous acts of kindness quickly grows into something much bigger. Along the way, they face challenges, resistance, and even their own doubts, but their determination never wavers.

This story is not just about laughter and pranks; it's about the power of human connection. Martha and George teach us that kindness is contagious, that even in a world full of challenges, we can all contribute to making it a little brighter. Whether it's by leaving a note of encouragement, organizing a picnic, or simply offering a smile to a stranger, each of us can play a part in this revolution of joy.

As you turn the pages of this book, you'll follow Martha and George on their mission to prove that no one is too old, too young, or too insignificant to make a difference. You'll see how their efforts inspire others, creating a chain reaction of kindness that changes their town forever.

So, grab a cup of tea, settle in, and join Martha and George in their delightful journey. You might just find that you, too, are ready to join the revolution.

Welcome to *The Joyful Revolution!*

Chapter 1: Old Friends, New Ideas

Chapter 2: The Birth of a Revolution

Chapter 3: Spreading Smiles, One Note at a Time

Chapter 4: The Mysterious Picnic

Chapter 5: A Bumpy Ride

Chapter 6: The Grumpy Neighbor

Chapter 7: A Glimmer of Success

Chapter 8: The Next Generation Joins In

Chapter 9: Tech Troubles

Chapter 10: Pranks with Purpose

Chapter 11: A Growing Movement

Chapter 12: Facing Resistance

Chapter 13: The Setback

Chapter 14: A Surprise Revival

Chapter 15: The Final Plan

Chapter 16: The Happiness Festival

Chapter 17: A World of Joy

Chapter 18: The Legacy Lives On

Chapter 1: Old Friends, New Ideas

Martha and George were two old friends who had known each other for as long as they could remember. Both in their late seventies, they met regularly at the same park, sitting on their favourite wooden bench under a large oak tree. The park, with its neatly trimmed grass, blooming flowers, and the sound of children playing in the distance, had become their little haven in a world that seemed to be changing too fast for their liking.

Martha, with her silver hair neatly tied into a bun and her flowery dress always spotless, was the more practical of the two. She had a way of noticing details that others might overlook, like how the flowers in the park bloomed earlier this year or how the old lampposts had been replaced with sleek, modern ones. George, on the other hand, was the more easy-going and humorous one, always ready with a joke or a funny story to lighten the mood. He often wore a tweed cap and carried a cane, though he didn't really need it. It was just part of his charm.

On this particular day, as the autumn leaves gently fell around them, Martha and George sat side by side, watching the world go by. It had become something of a routine for them—meeting in the park, reminiscing about the good old days, and sharing thoughts about how the world had changed. Today was no different.

"I don't know, George," Martha sighed, her eyes following a group of young people walking by, all with their heads bent over their phones. "Things aren't like they used to be. People don't talk to each other anymore. Everyone's in such a hurry."

George chuckled softly. "Ah, Martha, you sound like my grandmother! But you're right, though. Things have changed. Back in our day, if you wanted to talk to someone, you walked over to their house or met them at the local café. Now, people send messages through those blinking screens. It's not the same."

Martha nodded. "Exactly! I remember when we used to have real conversations. You'd meet someone at the market, and you'd talk for hours. You knew your neighbours, their children, their stories. Now, everyone's too busy to even smile at each other."

The two friends sat in silence for a moment, lost in their memories. Martha's mind wandered back to her childhood, growing up in a small village where everyone knew everyone. Life had been slower then, simpler. There had been a sense of community, of belonging, that seemed to be missing now. She missed the days when people took the time to care for one another, to help each other out without expecting anything in return.

George, too, was thinking about the past. He remembered his youth fondly—the days spent playing in the streets with his friends, the neighbourhood gatherings, and the warmth that seemed to fill the air. People had laughed more back then, he thought. There had been a joy in the little things—sharing a meal, telling a story, or simply sitting together and watching the world go by.

"I miss the laughter," George said quietly, breaking the silence. "People don't laugh as much as they used to. Everyone's so serious now, always worried about something."

Martha smiled gently. "You're right, George. I've noticed that too. It's like everyone's chasing something, but they don't even know what it is. They've forgotten how to be happy with what they have."

George turned to look at her, his eyes twinkling with a mischievous light. "You know, Martha, we could change that."

Martha raised an eyebrow, intrigued. "Oh? And how exactly do you propose we do that, George? You want to go around teaching people how to be happy?"

George chuckled again, leaning back on the bench. "Why not? We're two old folks with nothing but time on our hands. We could start small, do little things to remind people what joy feels like. You know, spread a bit of happiness."

Martha laughed softly, shaking her head. "You and your wild ideas, George. But..." She paused, thinking it over. "Maybe you're onto something. The world could use a bit more joy. And who better to spread it than two old folks who've seen it all?"

The idea, though lighthearted at first, began to take root in their minds. Martha and George had both lived long, full lives. They had seen the world change in ways they couldn't have imagined when they were younger. They had witnessed the rise of technology, the fast pace of modern life, and the increasing disconnect between people. But they had also experienced the beauty of simpler times, the warmth of human connection, and the happiness that came from the little things.

As they sat there, watching the world rush by, they began to talk more seriously about their idea. What if they could bring back some of that happiness? What if they could remind people that joy wasn't something you had to chase after, but something that could be found in the small moments of everyday life?

"Well," Martha said thoughtfully, "if we're going to do this, we'll need a plan."

George grinned. "Oh, I've got plenty of ideas, don't you worry about that. We could start with something simple. Leave little notes around the park, with kind words or funny messages. Something to make people smile."

Martha nodded. "Yes, I like that. We could write things like 'Have a beautiful day' or 'You are loved'. It doesn't have to be anything big, just enough to brighten someone's day."

"And," George added, his eyes gleaming with excitement, "we could bake some biscuits and hand them out to people as they walk by. You know, like they used to do at those church bazaars. Everyone loves a good biscuit."

Martha laughed. "Of course you'd think of biscuits! But that's a good idea. Simple, thoughtful, and it brings people together."

The more they talked, the more excited they became about their plan. It wasn't going to be a grand, world-changing mission. They weren't looking to fix all the problems of the modern world. But they could start small, right here in their own community, with small acts of kindness that could make a big difference.

As they continued brainstorming, they realised that the key to happiness wasn't in material things or in the latest gadgets. It was in the connections between people, in the way they treated each other, and in the little moments of joy that often went unnoticed.

"You know," Martha said after a while, "I think people have forgotten how to slow down. Everything's so fast these days—fast food, fast communication, fast living. But happiness isn't something you can rush. It comes from slowing down, taking the time to appreciate the world around you."

George nodded in agreement. "That's exactly it. People are so busy trying to get somewhere that they forget to enjoy the journey. Maybe we can remind them of that."

The sun was beginning to set, casting a warm, golden glow over the park. Martha and George sat in comfortable silence for a few moments, watching the colours change in the sky. The idea of spreading happiness, though it had started as a joke, now felt like something they could really do. They didn't need to change the world; they just needed to bring a little more joy into it, one small act at a time.

"Well, George," Martha said with a smile, "it looks like we've got ourselves a mission."

George grinned, tipping his cap to her. "A mission to spread happiness. I like the sound of that."

They stood up from the bench, their old bones creaking a little as they did. But they felt lighter than they had in years, filled with a renewed sense of purpose. As they slowly made their way out of the park, they couldn't help but feel excited about what lay ahead. It wasn't often that two old friends like them got the chance to start something new. But here they were, on the brink of an adventure, ready to bring a little bit of joy back into the world.

As they walked, Martha turned to George with a thoughtful expression. "You know, George, we can't do this all on our own. If we really want to make a difference, we'll need to get others involved. Maybe we can encourage people to join us, to do their own little acts of kindness."

George nodded. "That's a good idea. The more people we can get on board, the bigger impact we'll have. And who knows? Maybe our little revolution will spread."

Martha chuckled. "A revolution, is it? I suppose we could call it that. A revolution of joy."

And so, with that thought in mind, Martha and George began to hatch their plan. They would start small—just the two of them, leaving notes and handing out biscuits. But they hoped that, in time, their mission would grow. Maybe others would see the value in slowing down, in connecting with one another, and in finding joy in the little things. Maybe, just maybe, their simple acts of kindness would spread, creating a ripple effect that would touch more lives than they could ever imagine.

As they parted ways that evening, both Martha and George felt a sense of excitement they hadn't felt in years. They had found a new purpose, a way to make a difference in a world that sometimes felt too big and too complicated. And as they headed home, they couldn't wait to see where this new adventure would take them.

The Joyful Revolution had officially begun.

Chapter 2: The Birth of a Revolution

The idea had been planted, and like all good ideas, it started to grow. Martha and George couldn't stop thinking about it. The more they talked, the more excited they became about the possibility of spreading joy in their little town. What had started as a casual conversation during one of their usual park meetings was now turning into something bigger—something that felt real. They didn't want to change the world, but they did want to make a difference, even if it was just for a few people at a time.

It all began with their mutual sense of frustration over how the world had changed, how everything seemed so rushed, and how people seemed to have lost sight of the little things that made life beautiful. But now, they had decided to do something about it. They were going to start a revolution—a Joyful Revolution.

The next day, Martha and George met at George's house. George's place was as quirky as he was, with its mismatched furniture, cluttered shelves, and an air of comfortable disarray. His garden, though a bit overgrown, had a charm of its own, with old gnomes and wind chimes scattered about, and it was here, in a small shed at the back of the garden, that the two friends decided to set up their "headquarters." The shed, which had once been George's workshop, was filled with old tools, jars of screws and nails, and a layer of dust that showed it hadn't been used for anything serious in years. But to Martha and George, it was perfect.

"This'll do just fine," George said, dusting off an old wooden table that was tucked in the corner. "We can sit here, plan our missions, and no one will be the wiser."

Martha looked around the shed, trying to imagine it as the nerve centre of their joyful operation. "It's a bit dusty," she said, wrinkling her nose, "but I suppose it has character."

George chuckled. "Character is exactly what we need for this. This is where it all starts—the birth of The Joyful Revolution."

Martha smiled at his enthusiasm. "All right, George. So, what's our first plan? How do we start spreading joy?"

George sat down on a wooden stool and scratched his chin thoughtfully. "Well, we need to keep it simple to start. We're not young anymore, Martha, so we don't want to wear ourselves out with anything too big right off the bat. I say we start with something small, something easy."

Martha, always the practical one, nodded. "What about small acts of kindness? You know, things that don't take much effort but could make someone's day a little brighter. Like leaving cheerful notes in places where people might find them—on park benches, at bus stops, in cafés."

George's eyes lit up. "Now you're talking! I like that idea. It's simple, and it'll catch people by surprise. Imagine sitting down on a bench and finding a little note that says, 'You're doing great!' or 'Smile, it's a beautiful day!' People would love that."

Martha smiled, already feeling the excitement of their plan building inside her. "Yes, exactly! We could make the notes personal and thoughtful, something to make people feel seen, even if just for a moment."

George leaned forward, his mischievous grin spreading across his face. "And what if we added a bit of fun to it? You know me, Martha, I can't resist a little harmless prank now and then. What if we leave notes that say something like, 'You've just been recruited to The Joyful Revolution,' and see if anyone plays along?"

Martha raised an eyebrow but couldn't help but laugh. "George, you and your pranks! I don't know if people will understand what we're trying to do if we make it too much of a joke."

"Oh, come on," George said with a wink. "People need to laugh more. We can mix in some funny notes with the kind ones. Keep them on their toes."

Martha thought about it for a moment. George did have a point. In a world that often took itself too seriously, a bit of humour could go a long way. "All right, fine," she said with a playful smile. "But nothing too outrageous, George. We want to spread joy, not confuse people."

"Deal," George said, holding out his hand to shake on it.

With their plan starting to take shape, they began to gather supplies. Martha, ever the organiser, brought over a stack of colourful paper and some markers. George found an old box in his shed where they could store the notes once they were ready. They sat together in the shed, writing messages by hand, each one different from the last. Some were simple and sweet: *"You are loved,"* or *"Have a wonderful day."* Others had a bit of George's trademark humour: *"You've just been recruited to The Joyful Revolution. Your mission: Smile more."*

The shed buzzed with excitement as the pile of notes grew. Every now and then, George would look over at Martha and grin, as if to say, *"Can you believe we're doing this?"* And Martha, for her part, was just as thrilled. It had been a long time since she had felt this kind of excitement, this sense of purpose. The idea of spreading joy, of reminding people that happiness was still out there, filled her with a sense of hope she hadn't felt in years.

A few days later, their first "mission" was ready to go. The sun was shining brightly as Martha and George set out to distribute their notes. Armed with a small bag filled with their cheerful messages, they decided to start in the park where they always met. It felt fitting somehow—this was where the idea had first been born, and now it was time to put it into action.

They moved slowly, as old age often required, but there was an undeniable spring in their steps. Martha, with her careful precision, placed the notes neatly on benches, tucking them under the edge so they wouldn't blow away. George, meanwhile, couldn't resist the temptation to add a bit of flair to his placements. He left notes on top of trash bins, slipped one under a café chair, and even wedged one into the door of the post office.

As they worked, they couldn't help but imagine the reactions of the people who would find their notes. Maybe a tired mother would sit down on a bench, exhausted from her day, and find a note that reminded her that she was doing a great job. Maybe a grumpy office worker, rushing to catch the bus, would pause for a moment and smile when they found a note telling them to *"Remember to breathe."*

They continued like this for most of the morning, walking through the town, leaving their little pieces of joy wherever they could. It was a simple act, but it felt good—like they were part of something bigger than themselves. By the time they had finished, both Martha and George were tired but happy.

As they sat down on a bench to rest, George turned to Martha with a grin. "Well, that's the first mission complete. What do you think?"

Martha smiled, her face glowing with satisfaction. "I think we've done something good today, George. Even if only one person finds one of those notes and it makes them smile, it will have been worth it."

George nodded. "Exactly. That's how revolutions start, isn't it? With small things. Little acts that build up over time."

Martha laughed. "You're really set on calling this a revolution, aren't you?"

George winked. "Of course! A revolution of joy. And this is only the beginning, my dear Martha."

They sat together in silence for a while, watching the people pass by, wondering if anyone had already found one of their notes. Martha's mind was racing with ideas for their next mission, while George, ever the prankster, was already thinking of ways to add more fun to their future plans.

As the sun began to set, Martha and George slowly made their way back to George's house, feeling accomplished but also eager for what lay ahead. The Joyful Revolution had officially begun, and they couldn't wait to see where it would take them. The shed, once a dusty old space filled with forgotten tools, was now a symbol of their mission—a place where ideas were born, and plans were made.

Over the next few days, they kept an eye on the town, curious to see if anyone would notice their little acts of kindness. They watched from afar as people sat down on the benches where they had left notes, or entered the café where they had placed a few on the tables. They didn't expect any grand reactions, but they hoped that at least a few people would take a moment to smile.

And then, something unexpected happened. One afternoon, while Martha and George were sitting in the park, they noticed a woman sitting on the bench where they had placed one of their notes. She picked it up, read it, and smiled. But instead of simply putting it back or taking it with her, she did something that neither Martha nor George had expected—she pulled a small notebook out of her bag, tore out a page, and wrote her own message. Then, she placed it on the bench, next to the original note, before walking away.

Martha and George exchanged glances, their hearts racing with excitement. Had they just witnessed the birth of something bigger than they had anticipated? Maybe, just maybe, their little revolution was starting to spread.

"Well, George," Martha said, her voice filled with wonder, "it looks like we've got ourselves a movement."

George grinned, his eyes twinkling with mischief. "The Joyful Revolution, Martha. And it's only just begun."

With this small victory under their belts, Martha and George knew that their mission had truly begun. They had taken their first step toward spreading joy, and now there was no turning back. The Joyful Revolution was officially in motion, and as they sat in their shed that evening, brainstorming new ideas and laughing about their success, they couldn't help but feel that the best was yet to come.

The birth of their revolution had been simple, but its potential felt limitless. And as they prepared for their next mission, they knew one thing for certain: this was only the beginning.

Chapter 3: Spreading Smiles, One Note at a Time

The morning air was crisp and cool as Martha and George set off on their next mission. Their small bag was stuffed with sticky notes—bright pinks, yellows, and greens, all scribbled with kind, funny, and uplifting messages. Some of the notes were heartfelt: *"You are enough, just as you are,"* while others reflected George's playful spirit: *"Warning: This note contains a smile."* Together, they had spent the previous evening in George's shed, their little headquarters, coming up with an assortment of messages that they hoped would brighten people's days. Now, it was time to put their plan into action.

Both of them were a little nervous, not entirely sure how people would react to their anonymous act of kindness. Would the notes be ignored? Would people find them strange? Or, worst of all, would they be thrown away without a second thought? But despite their worries, there was an excitement that neither of them could deny. They were ready to make a difference, even if it was a small one.

Their first stop was the park—the same place where their idea for *The Joyful Revolution* had been born. It felt fitting to start here, in the place where they had spent so many afternoons talking about life, laughing, and imagining a simpler, more joyful world. The park was still quiet this early in the day, with only a few joggers and dog walkers out and about.

Martha, ever the planner, had already thought of where they should leave their notes. She carefully placed a few on the backs of benches, where people would see them when they sat down. George, on the other hand, was a bit more creative in his approach. He stuck one on the side of a rubbish bin with a message that read, *"Don't let this be the only thing that gets picked up today. Smile, you're wonderful!"*

Martha rolled her eyes at him, but she couldn't help but laugh. George's light-heartedness was infectious, and it balanced out her more serious nature perfectly.

As they moved through the park, they placed notes wherever they could: on lamp posts, at the base of trees, and even on the swings in the playground. Some of the messages were simple reminders to slow down and enjoy the moment: *"Take a deep breath and enjoy the view."* Others were playful prompts: *"Tag, you're it! Now go spread some joy."*

When they were done with the park, they moved on to other parts of the town. The bus stop was next, where Martha carefully placed a note on one of the benches: *"Waiting for the bus? How about waiting for a smile too?"* George, not to be outdone, stuck another on the glass of the bus shelter: *"This bus is heading straight to Happiness. Better hop on!"*

As the morning went on, they visited the local café, the library, and even the post office, leaving a trail of sticky notes behind them. Each time they stuck a note down, they couldn't help but imagine who might find it, and how they would react. Would a tired worker on their lunch break be cheered up by a funny message? Would a stressed student at the library smile when they found a note saying, *"You've got this!"*?

Martha and George didn't expect to see anyone actually find the notes; after all, the whole point was to be anonymous. But as they wandered through the town, something unexpected happened. They began to notice people reading the notes. A young woman at the bus stop picked up one of Martha's notes, her face lighting up as she read it. She tucked it into her bag with a smile, as if she wanted to keep the little piece of joy for herself. An older man, sitting on a bench in the park, chuckled when he found one of George's cheekier messages. He looked around, as if trying to figure out who had left it, but there was no one in sight.

Martha and George watched these moments from a distance, trying not to be seen. Every time they witnessed someone reacting to one of their notes, it filled them with a sense of accomplishment. It was working. Their simple little plan was actually working.

As they continued their mission, not all the reactions were what they had hoped for. Some people seemed puzzled when they found the notes, frowning slightly as they read the messages. One man picked up a note that read, *"You are capable of amazing things,"* and stared at it for a few moments before crumpling it up and tossing it in the bin. George winced when he saw that.

"Well, you can't win them all," he said with a shrug, trying to hide his disappointment.

Martha patted his arm. "It's all right, George. Not everyone's going to get it. But look at all the people who did. That's what matters."

George nodded, knowing she was right. For every person who dismissed the notes, there were plenty of others who smiled, chuckled, or pocketed the little messages of joy. It wasn't about reaching everyone, just about making a difference for those who were open to it.

By lunchtime, Martha and George were sitting in the park, watching people pass by, their work for the day done. They had left notes all over town, and now it was time to see how people reacted. As they sipped from their thermos of tea, they saw a woman sitting on one of the benches, picking up one of their notes. She smiled softly as she read it, then pulled out her phone and took a picture of it before placing it back for someone else to find.

"I think we're onto something here, Martha," George said, a grin spreading across his face. "People are actually enjoying this."

Martha smiled, feeling a warmth spread through her chest. "I think so too, George. And this is just the beginning."

They sat in comfortable silence for a while, watching the world go by. The sun was shining, the birds were singing, and there was a lightness in the air that hadn't been there before. Maybe it was just their own excitement, or maybe it was something bigger—a sense that they had started something, even if it was small, that had the potential to grow.

That evening, back in George's shed, they reflected on the day's success.

"We really did it, didn't we?" George said, leaning back in his chair with a satisfied grin. "We actually spread some joy today."

Martha nodded, feeling a sense of pride wash over her. "It feels good, doesn't it? Knowing that we've made even a small difference in someone's day."

George leaned forward, his eyes twinkling with mischief. "But we can't stop here, Martha. Now that we know it works, we've got to keep going. We've got to think bigger."

Martha raised an eyebrow, amused by his enthusiasm. "Bigger, George? How much bigger are you thinking?"

George's grin widened. "I don't know yet. But I'm thinking we don't just stick to notes. What if we start doing other things? Little surprises that people don't expect. We could leave flowers on people's doorsteps, or pay for someone's coffee at the café."

Martha's mind started racing with ideas. George was right—there was so much more they could do. They had only scratched the surface with their notes, but the possibilities were endless. Small acts of kindness, little gestures of joy, things that didn't cost much but could mean the world to someone. They could make their town a little brighter, one act at a time.

As the days went by, Martha and George continued their mission. Every morning, they would meet at the shed, their "headquarters," and plan out their day's activities. Some days, they stuck to leaving notes—now with even more variety in their messages. Other days, they would leave little gifts for people to find: a flower on a park bench, a book left on a bus stop with a note that said, *"Take me, I'm yours,"* or even a small bag of homemade biscuits with a tag that read, *"Baked with love."*

Each time they went out, they watched as people discovered their surprises. Some were confused at first, unsure of what to make of the random acts of kindness. But most people smiled, some even laughed, and a few were visibly touched by the gestures.

Martha and George never revealed themselves as the masterminds behind these small acts of joy. They didn't want the credit. They just wanted to see the happiness it brought to others. That was enough for them.

One particularly memorable moment happened on a quiet Sunday afternoon. Martha and George had left several notes scattered around the café. As they sat in the corner, sipping their tea and pretending to read the newspaper, they saw a young couple find one of the notes. The message simply said, *"You are loved."* The woman smiled as she showed it to her partner, who then leaned over and gave her a kiss on the cheek.

George nudged Martha with his elbow. "See that? That's what it's all about. It's not just the note—it's the little moment of joy it creates."

Martha nodded, her heart swelling with pride. It wasn't much, but in a world that often felt cold and disconnected, these small moments of connection, of shared joy, felt incredibly important. And the best part was, they were doing it together. Two old friends, united in their mission to make the world a little brighter, one note, one smile, one small act of kindness at a time.

By the end of the week, Martha and George had fully embraced their roles as bringers of joy. Their "Joyful Revolution" was well underway, and the excitement they felt had only grown. They had seen firsthand how a simple message or a small gesture could brighten someone's day, and they were eager to keep going. The town felt a little bit warmer, a little bit friendlier, and they liked to think that their efforts had something to do with it.

As they sat in their shed, surrounded by sticky notes, pens, and scraps of paper, they began brainstorming their next big idea.

"What's next, George?" Martha asked, her eyes gleaming with anticipation.

George leaned back in his chair, a mischievous smile playing on his lips. "Oh, I've got a few ideas up my sleeve. But you'll have to wait and see."

Martha chuckled, knowing that whatever George had in mind, it would be something fun and unexpected. After all, that was the essence of their revolution—spreading joy in ways that were surprising and delightful.

And so, with their spirits high and their determination stronger than ever, Martha and George prepared for their next mission. The Joyful Revolution was just getting started.

Chapter 4: The Mysterious Picnic

It was a breezy Saturday morning when Martha and George came up with their quirkiest idea yet. They were sitting in George's shed, as usual, brainstorming their next move for *The Joyful Revolution*. The shed was now filled with remnants of their past activities—scraps of sticky notes, pens, and even a collection of little trinkets they had left around town in the past week. The success of their note-spreading mission had given them a fresh surge of excitement, and they were eager to do something bigger, something that would bring people together in a more personal way.

"What if we threw a picnic?" George said suddenly, his eyes lighting up with excitement.

Martha, sitting across from him, raised an eyebrow. "A picnic?"

"Yeah, a picnic! But not just any picnic—a mysterious one," George continued, clearly getting carried away with his idea. "We set up a spread in the park, no invitations, no announcements, nothing. We just put everything out there and see who turns up."

Martha thought about it for a moment. "So, you're saying we should just... show up, set up a picnic, and hope people join in?"

George nodded enthusiastically. "Exactly! Think about it, Martha. It's a way to get people to step out of their usual routine, to take a break from their phones and their busy lives, and just enjoy a simple moment with others. No pressure, no expectations, just a chance for people to connect. Face-to-face, like in the good old days."

Martha smiled, feeling the familiar warmth of excitement bubbling up inside her. George always had a knack for coming up with these offbeat ideas, and she had to admit, there was something charming about the simplicity of it. A picnic in the park, with no agenda other than bringing people together. In a world that seemed increasingly disconnected, it felt like the perfect next step in their mission.

"All right," she said, nodding in agreement. "Let's do it. Let's throw a mysterious picnic."

The plan was set in motion the following day. Martha and George made a list of everything they would need—blankets, a variety of food, drinks, and of course, a few of George's quirky touches to make the whole thing more fun. They spent the morning shopping for picnic essentials: sandwiches, crisps, fruit, and a selection of homemade treats that Martha had baked herself the night before. George, true to form, insisted on bringing a collection of random, whimsical items—colourful paper hats, a deck of cards, and even an old portable radio he found in his attic.

"This picnic is going to be one for the books," George said as they loaded everything into the back of Martha's car.

Martha chuckled. "Let's just hope people actually show up."

They arrived at the park in the early afternoon, the sun shining brightly overhead. The park was one of their favourite spots, a peaceful, open space with plenty of trees and a large grassy area perfect for a picnic. As they began unpacking, they chose a spot under the shade of a tall oak tree, spreading out several blankets to create a cozy, inviting space. Martha arranged the food on one of the blankets, while George set up the portable radio, tuning it to a station that played soft, cheerful music.

The idea was simple: set everything up and wait. No signs, no explanations, just a welcoming space for anyone who happened to pass by.

As they finished preparing, they sat back and admired their work. It looked perfect—inviting, warm, and full of the kind of charm that Martha and George hoped would draw people in. Now, all they had to do was wait and see if their mysterious picnic would attract any curious onlookers.

At first, the park was quiet. A few joggers passed by, and a couple of families strolled through with their children, but no one stopped to investigate the picnic. Martha and George sat on the blankets, trying to look casual as they ate their sandwiches and sipped lemonade. They weren't exactly nervous, but there was a sense of anticipation hanging in the air. Would anyone actually join them? Or would they end up having this picnic all by themselves?

After about twenty minutes, the first sign of curiosity appeared. A young couple walking their dog wandered over to the picnic area, their eyes lingering on the spread of food and the colourful blankets. They didn't say anything at first, just exchanged glances, clearly unsure whether they were allowed to join in.

George, never one to miss an opportunity, gave them a friendly wave. "Hello there! Care for a snack?"

The couple looked surprised at the invitation, but after a moment of hesitation, they smiled and made their way over. The woman knelt down to pet the dog, while the man asked, "Is this... a public picnic?"

Martha smiled warmly. "It's whatever you want it to be. We just thought it would be nice to set something up and see who wanted to join."

"Well, that's lovely!" the woman said, reaching for a sandwich. "You don't see this kind of thing very often."

As they sat down and introduced themselves, Martha and George felt a sense of relief. The first guests had arrived, and it was already shaping up to be a success. They chatted with the couple about the town, the park, and the importance of slowing down to enjoy life's simple pleasures. The conversation was easy, lighthearted, and natural—just the kind of interaction Martha and George had hoped for.

Before long, more people began to trickle in. A pair of elderly ladies on their afternoon walk stopped by, drawn in by the sight of the picnic. They joined Martha and George, happily accepting some tea and biscuits. Then, a group of teenagers arrived, curious about the gathering. At first, they hung back, unsure if they should get involved, but George waved them over with a grin.

"Come on, don't be shy! There's plenty of food to go around."

The teenagers laughed, grabbed some crisps, and sat down on the blankets. They seemed a bit awkward at first, unsure of how to interact with the mix of people already gathered, but it didn't take long for them to relax. Soon, they were joking with George and even playing a game of cards with the elderly ladies, who turned out to be quite competitive.

As the afternoon wore on, more and more people joined the picnic. Some brought their own snacks to contribute, while others simply enjoyed the food Martha and George had provided. It was a beautiful mix of people—families, couples, friends, and strangers, all coming together in an unexpected way. Conversations flowed naturally, laughter filled the air, and for a little while, it felt as if the outside world didn't exist.

Martha and George sat back, watching it all unfold with a sense of wonder. This was exactly what they had hoped for—a spontaneous gathering that brought people together in a way that felt effortless and genuine. They hadn't forced anything; they had simply created a space for connection, and people had responded.

At one point, a man in his thirties approached Martha, looking around at the scene with a curious expression. "What's the occasion?" he asked.

Martha smiled. "No occasion. Just a picnic."

The man raised an eyebrow. "Just a picnic?"

"Yep," Martha said, offering him a sandwich. "We thought it would be nice to have a picnic and see if anyone wanted to join."

The man chuckled, clearly amused. "That's... unexpected. But kind of brilliant."

He sat down on one of the blankets, taking a bite of the sandwich. After a few moments, he turned to Martha again. "You know, I can't remember the last time I sat in a park and just... talked to strangers. It's nice."

Martha nodded, feeling a sense of satisfaction. "That's what we were hoping for. Sometimes it feels like people are so disconnected these days, always rushing from one thing to the next. We wanted to create a moment for people to slow down and enjoy each other's company."

The man smiled, clearly impressed. "Well, mission accomplished."

As the afternoon turned into evening, the atmosphere at the picnic grew even more relaxed. People who had arrived as strangers were now chatting like old friends, sharing stories and laughter. Some of the teenagers had started a game of frisbee, inviting others to join in, while the elderly ladies were deep in conversation with a young couple about their travels.

George, ever the life of the party, had put on his paper hat and was encouraging others to do the same. It wasn't long before half the people at the picnic were wearing the silly hats, laughing and posing for photos. Even Martha, who usually preferred to stay in the background, couldn't resist joining in on the fun.

As they looked around at the crowd they had brought together, Martha and George felt a deep sense of accomplishment. This wasn't just about spreading joy anymore—this was about building a community, even if just for a few hours. People from all walks of life had come together, connected by something as simple as a picnic in the park. There were no barriers, no distractions, just face-to-face interaction in its purest form.

By the time the sun began to set, the picnic was winding down. People started packing up their things, saying their goodbyes, and thanking Martha and George for the wonderful afternoon. Some of them even asked if there would be another picnic in the future, to which George enthusiastically replied, "Definitely!"

As the last of the guests left, Martha and George sat on the blankets, watching the sun dip below the horizon. The park was quiet again, but the echoes of laughter and conversation still lingered in the air. They had done it. They had brought people together, not through grand gestures or elaborate plans, but through something as simple and spontaneous as a picnic.

"I think today was a success," George said, leaning back and smiling at the sky.

Martha nodded, feeling a sense of peace. "Yeah. I think so too."

And with that, The Joyful Revolution continued to grow, one small, mysterious picnic at a time.

Chapter 5: A Bumpy Ride

Martha and George were riding high on the success of their picnic. The *Joyful Revolution* was off to a strong start, and they were more determined than ever to spread joy in their community. Their spontaneous picnic had brought together strangers from all walks of life, and the sense of connection and laughter that filled the park had given them a renewed sense of purpose. Now, they were ready for their next idea—a grand, old-fashioned bicycle ride through town.

It was George who first proposed the idea, sitting in the shed one evening, still buzzing from the picnic's success. "What if we organized a bike ride?" he said, grinning. "A real throwback, you know? No fancy gear or professional cyclists. Just a bunch of people, riding through town on their old bikes, ringing bells and waving at everyone. It would be fun and a little bit silly, which is exactly what this town needs!"

Martha, who had always loved riding her bicycle as a child, immediately lit up at the suggestion. "That sounds perfect! A nice, slow ride through town, where people can join us if they want. We can decorate our bikes and maybe even hand out some little treats along the way."

George's eyes twinkled mischievously. "And we could wear some ridiculous outfits. Something old-timey, like tweed and hats with feathers."

Martha laughed, already imagining the scene. "You're impossible, George. But I like it."

With their plan set, they spent the next few days getting everything ready. Martha dusted off her old bicycle, a charming, slightly worn-out blue one that she hadn't ridden in years. George, on the other hand, had to borrow a bike from his neighbor since his own was in such bad shape that it barely resembled a functional vehicle. He managed to find an old, rickety bike with a basket on the front, which he insisted would be perfect for the ride.

To add to the fun, they decided to put up some handmade posters around town, inviting people to join their old-fashioned bike ride. The posters were simple but quirky, featuring hand-drawn illustrations of bicycles with smiling faces and the slogan: *"Join the Joyful Revolution: A Bicycle Ride Through Town—Bring Your Bike, Your Bell, and Your Smile!"*

They taped the posters to lampposts, bus stops, and bulletin boards, hoping that their message would reach a few adventurous souls. They even mentioned the event at the local café, where they had become regulars since starting *The Joyful Revolution*. The café owner, a friendly woman named Mary, promised to spread the word to her customers.

The day of the bike ride arrived, and Martha and George were full of excitement. They met at the park, the same one where they had held their picnic, and began decorating their bikes with colourful streamers, small baskets of flowers, and even a few homemade flags that fluttered in the breeze. True to George's word, they had dressed in old-fashioned clothing—Martha in a light floral dress and a wide-brimmed hat, and George in a tweed jacket, complete with a cap that looked like it belonged in a 1920s film.

"This is going to be brilliant," George said, adjusting the feathers in his cap as he tested the bell on his bike. It gave a soft *ding*, which only made him smile more. "We're going to be the talk of the town."

Martha, carefully placing the last flower in her basket, nodded. "I hope so. Even if just a few people show up, it'll still be fun."

As the time for the ride approached, Martha and George stood by their bikes, watching the park's entrance expectantly. Slowly, a few people started trickling in—a couple of families with children, a small group of teenagers, and a few older folks who looked like they hadn't ridden a bike in years but were clearly up for the challenge. In total, about a dozen people showed up, which wasn't as many as Martha and George had hoped for, but it was enough to get the ride started.

"Not bad for our first bike ride," Martha said, giving George an encouraging smile.

"Yeah, it's a good start," George agreed, though he couldn't hide his slight disappointment. He had hoped for more riders, but he quickly shook off the feeling. After all, *The Joyful Revolution* wasn't about numbers—it was about spreading joy, no matter how many people joined in.

As the group set off, ringing their bells and laughing together, Martha felt a sense of freedom she hadn't experienced in years. The sun was shining, the air was warm, and the sound of the bicycle wheels turning on the pavement filled the streets with a sense of movement and energy. George led the way, waving at people they passed by, some of whom looked confused but smiled nonetheless.

Everything seemed perfect—until it wasn't.

Martha was riding ahead of George when she heard a strange clunking sound. She looked down at her bike and saw that the chain had come loose, causing her pedals to stop moving. Her bike wobbled, and she quickly steered it to the side of the road before coming to a complete stop.

"Oh no," she muttered, dismounting and kneeling down to inspect the chain. "I think it's broken."

George, who had been pedaling happily along, noticed Martha was no longer beside him. He turned around just in time to see her kneeling by the side of the road, looking at her bike in frustration. He circled back, his own bike wobbling dangerously as he tried to keep his balance. The bike he had borrowed wasn't exactly in great condition either.

"Everything all right?" George called out, pulling up beside her.

Martha shook her head. "The chain came off. I think it's broken. I can't pedal."

George looked at the chain and scratched his head. "Well, I'm no bike mechanic, but that doesn't look too good."

By now, the rest of the group had noticed the commotion and slowed down, gathering around Martha and George to see what was happening. One of the teenagers offered to take a look, crouching down to examine the chain. After a few minutes of fiddling, he stood up and shrugged. "It's busted. I don't think we can fix it here."

Martha sighed, feeling a wave of disappointment wash over her. "Great. So much for the ride."

George, however, wasn't about to let a broken bike ruin the day. "Come on, it's not the end of the world. You can hop on the back of my bike! It'll be like old times, when we used to give each other rides as kids."

Martha blinked at him, half-laughing at the absurdity of the idea. "George, your bike can barely hold you, let alone both of us."

George grinned. "Nonsense! It'll be fine. We'll wobble a bit, but it'll add to the adventure!"

Martha hesitated, but seeing George's mischievous smile made it hard to say no. She couldn't help but laugh. "All right, fine. Let's give it a try."

What followed was a comical disaster.

Martha climbed onto the back of George's already wobbly bike, clutching his shoulders for balance as he tried to pedal forward. The bike, never designed to hold two adults, lurched from side to side like a drunken goose. George strained to keep his balance, and the group behind them couldn't stop laughing at the sight.

"You're going to kill us, George!" Martha yelled, half-laughing and half-panicking as they swayed dangerously close to the curb.

"I've got this!" George called out, though his voice didn't sound quite as confident as his words. The bike teetered, wobbled, and finally tipped over, sending both Martha and George tumbling onto the grass beside the road.

The entire group burst into laughter, and even Martha and George couldn't help but join in. They lay on the grass, breathless from laughing, while their fellow riders gathered around, offering them a hand up.

"Well," George said, still chuckling as he dusted himself off, "that didn't go exactly as planned."

Martha, her face flushed from laughter, shook her head. "You think?"

Despite the setbacks, the group continued their ride, albeit at a slower pace. George ended up walking his bike for the rest of the journey, with Martha by his side, her broken bike leaning against her shoulder. They laughed at themselves, waving at the others as they rode past, and shared stories about their childhood misadventures on bikes.

Though fewer people had shown up than they had hoped, and though their ride had turned into a bit of a mess, Martha and George found joy in the imperfections. They laughed at their own clumsiness, at the broken bike, and at George's failed attempt to carry Martha on the back of his old, creaky bicycle.

By the time they reached the end of the ride, the sun was beginning to set, casting a warm, golden glow over the town. The group gathered for one last laugh, sharing stories of their own mishaps during the ride—bumped curbs, wobbly turns, and near collisions. Despite everything, they had enjoyed the ride, not because it had been smooth or perfect, but because it had been filled with laughter and good company.

Martha and George stood at the edge of the group, watching as people slowly started heading home, waving and thanking them for organizing the event. Even with all the chaos, the bike ride had been a success in its own way. It wasn't about the number of people or how well things went—it was about the moments of joy they had shared, the laughter they had sparked, and the community they were slowly building.

As they packed up their things and prepared to leave, George looked at Martha and grinned. "Well, that was a bumpy ride."

Martha laughed. "Yeah, but you know what? I think it was one of the most fun things we've done so far."

"Agreed," George said, still smiling. "And next time, maybe we'll actually manage to ride without falling off."

Martha rolled her eyes playfully. "We'll see."

And with that, they walked their bikes home, already brainstorming their next idea for The Joyful Revolution. They had learned an important lesson that day—not every attempt would be perfect, and not everything would go according to plan. But even in the face of mishaps and failures, there was always joy to be found.

They had fallen off their bikes, but they had gotten back up, laughing all the way.

Chapter 6: The Grumpy Neighbor

After the comical disaster of the bike ride, Martha and George found themselves more motivated than ever to continue their mission with *The Joyful Revolution*. Despite the hiccups along the way, they were starting to realize that even the smallest gestures of joy could have a profound impact, even if things didn't go as planned. But there was one person in particular who they knew needed a bit more than just smiles and laughter—Mr. Willis, their notoriously grumpy neighbor.

Mr. Willis had been the subject of neighborhood gossip for as long as Martha and George could remember. He was an older man who lived alone in a house that seemed as cold and unfriendly as he was. The garden was overgrown with weeds, the curtains were always drawn, and no one ever seemed to visit. He rarely left the house, except for occasional trips to the grocery store, and when he did, he was always scowling.

Whether it was the noise of children playing in the street or a dog barking in the middle of the night, Mr. Willis always found something to grumble about. He had once yelled at Martha for trimming her hedges too close to his property line, and George had been on the receiving end of one of Mr. Willis's tirades when his football accidentally ended up in the man's garden.

"He's like a bear with a sore head," George had said after that incident. "Always grumpy, always ready to snap at you."

Martha had nodded in agreement at the time, but now, as they sat at the kitchen table discussing their next move for *The Joyful Revolution*, she had a different thought.

"I think we should try to cheer up Mr. Willis," she said, tapping her finger thoughtfully on the table.

George raised an eyebrow. "Cheer up Mr. Willis? That's like trying to teach a cat to swim. Impossible."

Martha smiled. "Maybe. But isn't that the whole point of what we're doing? Bringing joy to people who need it the most? And I don't think anyone needs it more than Mr. Willis."

George sighed, leaning back in his chair. "I don't know, Martha. The man seems like he's determined to be miserable. What if he doesn't want to be cheered up?"

"Then we'll just have to try harder," Martha said, her eyes gleaming with determination. "There's got to be a way to get through to him."

The next morning, Martha and George put their plan into action. They decided to start small, hoping that a few simple gestures of kindness might chip away at Mr. Willis's tough exterior. After all, who could resist a nice, warm homemade pie?

Martha spent the morning baking a delicious apple pie, filling the kitchen with the sweet scent of cinnamon and baked apples. She wrapped it in a towel and placed it carefully in a basket, while George made sure to grab a bottle of cream to go with it.

"This will work," Martha said confidently as they walked over to Mr. Willis's house. "Who doesn't love pie?"

George, less convinced, shrugged. "I guess we'll find out."

They knocked on Mr. Willis's door, waiting anxiously as they heard footsteps approaching from inside. The door creaked open, revealing the familiar scowl of their neighbor.

"What do you want?" Mr. Willis grumbled, his brow furrowed in suspicion.

Martha smiled warmly. "We just wanted to bring you something. A little treat to brighten your day."

She held out the pie, but Mr. Willis didn't even glance at it. Instead, his scowl deepened.

"Is that apple pie?" he asked gruffly.

"Yes! Freshly baked this morning," Martha replied, still smiling.

Mr. Willis shook his head. "I'm allergic to apples."

Martha's face fell, and George stifled a chuckle beside her. "Oh, I'm so sorry, Mr. Willis! We had no idea."

The old man grumbled something under his breath, but it was clear he wasn't impressed by their efforts. "Well, you can keep it. I don't need it."

Martha quickly offered an apology, and the two of them retreated, feeling slightly defeated. As they walked back to their house, George couldn't help but laugh.

"Great start, Martha. We nearly poisoned him."

Martha rolled her eyes, though she couldn't help but smile at the absurdity of the situation. "Okay, so the pie was a disaster. But we'll try something else. We're not giving up that easily."

Over the next few days, Martha and George tried everything they could think of to bring a little joy into Mr. Willis's life. They left small gifts on his doorstep—a box of chocolates, a potted plant, even a pair of woolly socks for the chilly weather. But every time they saw Mr. Willis, he was just as grumpy as ever.

They also tried to engage him in conversation when they saw him outside, but their attempts were met with cold indifference. Mr. Willis would grunt in response to their greetings and quickly retreat back into his house, as though he couldn't get away from them fast enough.

George, ever the prankster, even suggested pulling a few harmless tricks to get Mr. Willis to crack a smile. "What if we leave a rubber chicken in his mailbox?" he suggested with a grin.

Martha shook her head, though she couldn't help but laugh at the image. "We're trying to cheer him up, not drive him insane."

But after several failed attempts to get through to their grumpy neighbor, even Martha was beginning to feel discouraged. It seemed like no matter what they did, Mr. Willis remained as closed off and irritable as ever. The man was like a fortress, and nothing they did seemed to breach his walls.

THE JOYFUL REVOLUTION

One afternoon, after another unsuccessful attempt at conversation, Martha and George sat on the front steps of their house, feeling dejected.

"Maybe we were wrong," Martha said quietly, her usual optimism dimmed. "Maybe Mr. Willis doesn't want joy in his life."

George, who had been unusually quiet, glanced over at her. "I don't think that's it. I think there's more to him than we realize."

Martha looked at him curiously. "What do you mean?"

George shrugged. "I don't know. I just have this feeling that he's not really as grumpy as he seems. Maybe he's just... lonely."

Martha considered this for a moment. "Lonely?"

"Yeah. Think about it. He's always alone. No one ever visits him, and he never seems to talk to anyone. Maybe he's just used to being by himself, and he doesn't know how to connect with people anymore."

Martha nodded slowly, realizing that George might be onto something. She had been so focused on trying to bring surface-level joy to Mr. Willis—pies, gifts, and friendly greetings—that she hadn't considered the possibility that what he really needed was something deeper.

The next day, Martha decided to take a different approach. Instead of bringing over a pie or leaving a gift on his doorstep, she knocked on Mr. Willis's door with nothing but a simple offer: a conversation.

Mr. Willis opened the door, his usual frown in place. "What now?" he grumbled.

Martha smiled, though this time her smile was softer, less about cheerfulness and more about understanding. "I was wondering if I could sit with you for a while. Just to talk. I've noticed that we've never really had a proper conversation, and I'd like to get to know you a little better."

Mr. Willis blinked, clearly taken aback by the offer. For a moment, he didn't say anything, just stared at her as though trying to figure out if she was serious. But then, much to Martha's surprise, he stepped aside and gestured for her to come in.

Martha entered the house, finding it much as she had imagined—dimly lit, with furniture that looked like it hadn't been used in years. The air was heavy with the scent of old books and dust, and the walls were lined with shelves filled with knick-knacks and framed photographs, though many of the frames were turned face down.

Mr. Willis led her to a small sitting room, where they both sat down. For a while, there was an awkward silence, but Martha didn't mind. She had expected this—it wasn't easy for someone like Mr. Willis to open up, especially after so many years of shutting people out.

Finally, after what felt like an eternity, Mr. Willis spoke.

"I'm not much for company," he muttered, staring at the floor.

"That's okay," Martha replied gently. "I'm not here to bother you. I just wanted to say hello, and maybe listen if you ever feel like talking."

Mr. Willis glanced at her, his eyes narrowing slightly as though he were trying to decide whether or not to trust her. But then he sighed and leaned back in his chair, his shoulders sagging with the weight of something unseen.

"Everyone thinks I'm just an old grouch," he said after a moment. "Always complaining, always angry. But that's not it."

Martha listened intently, sensing that this was the moment they had been waiting for.

Mr. Willis continued, his voice quiet but filled with emotion. "My wife passed away five years ago. Since then, it's just been me in this house. We never had kids, and I don't have any family nearby. I guess I just got used to being alone."

Martha's heart softened as she realized the depth of Mr. Willis's loneliness. It wasn't that he didn't want joy in his life—it was that he didn't know how to let it in anymore.

"I'm so sorry," she said softly. "I didn't know."

THE JOYFUL REVOLUTION

Mr. Willis nodded, his eyes distant. "No one does. I don't talk about it. I just... I don't know how to be around people anymore."

Martha reached out, placing a hand on his arm. "It's never too late to start."

For the first time since she had known him, Mr. Willis's scowl softened, and a faint smile tugged at the corners of his mouth.

In the days that followed, Martha and George made a point to visit Mr. Willis regularly. Sometimes they brought over dinner, other times they just sat and talked. Slowly but surely, the old man began to open up, sharing stories from his past and even laughing at some of George's silly jokes.

It wasn't an overnight transformation, and Mr. Willis still had his grumpy moments. But underneath it all, Martha and George could see that they had made a difference. What Mr. Willis had needed wasn't just cheerful gestures—it was genuine human connection, something that had been missing from his life for far too long.

As Martha and George walked home after one of their visits, George looked over at her and smiled. "You were right, you know."

"About what?" Martha asked.

"About Mr. Willis. He didn't need a pie or a prank—he just needed someone to listen."

Martha smiled, feeling a sense of satisfaction wash over her. "Sometimes, joy isn't about big gestures. It's about being there for someone when they need it the most."

And with that, they continued their walk, knowing that The Joyful Revolution had just taken another step forward—one small, meaningful step at a time.

Chapter 7: A Glimmer of Success

After their emotional breakthrough with Mr. Willis, Martha and George found themselves deep in thought. While their mission with *The Joyful Revolution* had been well-intentioned from the start, the experience with their grumpy neighbor had taught them an important lesson. Not everyone was waiting to be cheered up by grand gestures or elaborate plans. Sometimes, people needed something much simpler: a moment of kindness, a reminder that someone cared.

As they sat at the kitchen table the morning after one of their visits to Mr. Willis, the mood was more reflective than usual. Martha was staring at a piece of toast, absentmindedly spreading jam, while George, uncharacteristically quiet, toyed with a spoon.

"I've been thinking," Martha finally said, breaking the silence.

"Uh-oh," George teased lightly, though he didn't look up from his spoon.

Martha smiled but didn't let the joke distract her. "Maybe we're trying too hard."

George raised an eyebrow. "Trying too hard? To cheer people up?"

"Not exactly," Martha said, pausing to gather her thoughts. "I mean, we've been focusing on these big gestures—like baking pies, buying gifts, and all that. But maybe what people really need isn't something fancy. Maybe it's just something simple, something small that can brighten their day in the moment."

George considered this. "So... no more pie attempts?"

Martha chuckled. "No more pies for people who are allergic, that's for sure."

George grinned and sat up, now intrigued by her idea. "Okay, so what's the new plan?"

"I'm not entirely sure," Martha admitted, running her fingers through her hair. "But what if we just try something really small? Like giving people flowers?"

George blinked. "Flowers?"

"Yes, flowers!" Martha's eyes lit up as the idea began to take shape in her mind. "Think about it. Everyone loves flowers. They're beautiful, they're simple, and they don't require a lot of fuss. We could stand in the town square and hand them out to people. No strings attached, no complicated plan. Just a simple act of kindness."

George sat back, tapping his chin thoughtfully. "I don't know... Flowers sound kind of... well, ordinary. Will that really make a difference?"

Martha nodded firmly. "It's not about the flowers themselves. It's about the gesture. Sometimes, the smallest acts of kindness can have the biggest impact. People aren't expecting something huge—they just need a little reminder that the world can be kind."

George was quiet for a moment, but then a smile spread across his face. "Alright, I'm in. Flowers it is. Let's see if simplicity works."

The next day, Martha and George made their way to the town square, their arms filled with fresh bouquets of colorful flowers. They had spent the morning at the local florist, carefully selecting a mix of daisies, roses, tulips, and carnations. The sight of the vibrant blooms lifted their spirits instantly, and as they approached the bustling square, they felt a surge of excitement.

The town square was always a busy place, especially on weekends. Families strolled by with children in tow, couples held hands as they window-shopped, and elderly residents sat on benches, watching the world go by. The air was filled with the sounds of chatter, laughter, and the occasional honking of car horns. It was the perfect place for their next experiment.

As they set up a small table near the fountain, George looked around and nudged Martha. "Are you sure people are going to take these? What if they think we're trying to sell them something?"

Martha shrugged, though she felt a twinge of nervousness herself. "We'll just have to explain that they're free. No catches, no tricks. Just flowers."

George rolled his eyes playfully. "Sure, because people totally believe that things are free these days."

Martha laughed but pushed forward, arranging the flowers neatly on the table. They had made a small sign that read: *"Free Flowers – A Small Act of Kindness, No Strings Attached!"*

George grabbed a bouquet of daisies and held it up, practicing his smile. "Okay, who's going to be our first customer?"

Martha, scanning the square, spotted an older woman walking slowly past the fountain, her arms full of grocery bags. She looked tired, as though the weight of her shopping was taking a toll. Without hesitating, Martha picked up a small bouquet of carnations and approached the woman.

"Excuse me," she said, her voice warm and friendly. "Would you like some flowers? They're free. Just a little something to brighten your day."

The woman blinked, clearly surprised by the offer. She glanced from Martha to the flowers, her expression uncertain. "Free?"

"Yes," Martha said with a smile. "No catch, I promise. Just a small act of kindness."

For a moment, the woman hesitated, but then her face softened, and she reached out to take the bouquet. "Well, that's very kind of you. Thank you, dear."

As the woman walked away, her step seemed a little lighter, and Martha's heart swelled with satisfaction. She turned back to George, who had been watching from the table.

"One down," George said, grinning. "A hundred more to go."

THE JOYFUL REVOLUTION

As the day went on, more and more people stopped by the table, each one greeted with a smile and an offer of a free bouquet. Some were hesitant at first, like the older woman, but once they realized there were no hidden motives, they accepted the flowers with gratitude. Others were delighted from the start, their faces lighting up as they picked out their favorite blooms.

A young mother pushing a stroller paused to choose a small bunch of tulips, her toddler giggling as George handed him a daisy to hold. A group of teenagers passing by initially made jokes, but when Martha offered them each a flower, their teasing turned to genuine smiles as they tucked the blooms behind their ears or into their backpacks.

An elderly man sitting on a nearby bench watched the scene with quiet interest, and when Martha approached him with a single rose, he chuckled and accepted it with a nod. "It's been a long time since anyone gave me flowers," he said softly.

Martha smiled, her heart warming at his words. "You deserve them."

As the hours passed, something remarkable began to happen. People who had initially taken flowers in passing began to linger. Some stopped to chat with Martha and George, sharing stories about their day or their love for flowers. Others, who had seen the flowers being handed out from afar, came over just to see what was going on. The square, usually filled with people going about their business without much interaction, began to feel different—more alive, more connected.

At one point, a man in a suit who had been rushing through the square on his way to a meeting suddenly stopped in his tracks. He watched as a little girl ran up to the table and picked out a sunflower, her eyes wide with excitement.

"What's all this?" the man asked, curiosity in his voice.

George handed him a rose. "Just spreading a bit of joy. Would you like a flower?"

The man hesitated, clearly not used to receiving unexpected kindness. But then he smiled—a genuine, warm smile—and took the rose. "Well, you've brightened my day," he said before hurrying off, the rose held carefully in his hand.

As the afternoon wore on, Martha and George noticed something else: the mood of the square had shifted. Where there had once been a hurried energy, people were now moving a little more slowly, taking the time to look around and smile at each other. It was as though the simple act of giving away flowers had created a ripple effect, spreading a sense of calm and connection throughout the area.

A few people even came back to the table after receiving their flowers, not to take more, but just to say thank you.

One woman, who had initially taken a bouquet of daisies without much comment, returned an hour later with tears in her eyes. "I just wanted to say that this really meant a lot to me," she said softly. "It's been a tough week, and this small gesture reminded me that there's still kindness in the world."

Martha's throat tightened with emotion, and she reached out to give the woman a hug. "I'm so glad we could help."

By the time the sun began to set, Martha and George had given away almost all the flowers. As they packed up the table, their hearts were full. They hadn't set out that morning with grand expectations—just a hope that their small gesture might bring a little bit of joy to the town. But what they had experienced had been more powerful than they could have imagined.

As they walked home, George couldn't help but grin. "Well, I think it's safe to say that flowers were a hit."

Martha smiled, feeling a renewed sense of purpose. "I told you. Sometimes the simplest things can make the biggest difference."

George nodded, his usual teasing tone replaced with sincerity. "You're right, Martha. Today was... well, it was amazing. I think this might be the start of something big."

That evening, as they sat together in the living room, reflecting on the day's events, Martha felt a sense of peace wash over her. *The Joyful Revolution* wasn't just about grand gestures or complex plans—it was about moments like today, where small, sincere acts of kindness could change someone's outlook, even if just for a little while.

"I feel like we're finally getting somewhere," George said, his voice thoughtful. "Not just with the flowers, but with the whole idea of what we're doing. It's not about trying to change the world overnight. It's about little moments, little gestures that remind people they're not alone."

Martha nodded, her heart swelling with pride. "Exactly. One flower at a time."

And with that, they knew that The Joyful Revolution had truly begun—not with a bang, but with a quiet, beautiful glimmer of success.

Chapter 8: The Next Generation Joins In

After the success of their flower giveaway in the town square, Martha and George felt invigorated. The simplicity of their gesture had been powerful enough to touch the hearts of those they encountered, and it had reassured them that *The Joyful Revolution* was on the right track. What they didn't anticipate, however, was just how far-reaching their efforts would become.

It started quietly, as most revolutions do. A few people in town spoke to their friends and neighbors, sharing stories of the mysterious older couple who had brightened their day with flowers. Soon, word spread, and before Martha and George knew it, more and more people were recognizing them as they went about their daily errands.

"You're the ones with the flowers, aren't you?" a shopkeeper asked one day when Martha was buying milk.

"I heard about you two!" a woman exclaimed in the park, waving excitedly as she passed by with her dog. "Keep it up! You're doing something wonderful!"

While these small encounters warmed their hearts, neither Martha nor George could have predicted what would happen next.

It was a sunny afternoon when a group of local kids approached their home, giggling nervously as they shuffled outside the gate. Martha and George were sitting on their front porch, enjoying a cup of tea and admiring their garden, when they noticed the group lingering by the fence.

"There's quite a crowd forming," George muttered, lowering his teacup as he squinted at the kids.

Martha glanced over, chuckling softly. "Looks like we have visitors."

The children, perhaps ten or twelve in number, ranged in age from around six to thirteen. Their leader, a boy of about twelve, finally worked up the courage to open the gate and approach the porch. He walked up the path with a mix of determination and nervousness, and the others followed closely behind.

"Uh... excuse me," the boy said, scratching his head. "Are you two the people who are making everyone happy with flowers and stuff?"

Martha and George exchanged a glance before George nodded, smiling kindly. "That's us. Why do you ask?"

The boy straightened up, encouraged by George's warm response. "Well, we've been hearing a lot about you guys, and we were wondering if we could, you know, help out?"

Martha raised an eyebrow, clearly surprised. "Help out? You mean you want to join *The Joyful Revolution*?"

The kids all nodded enthusiastically, and one of the younger girls piped up, "Yeah! We want to do nice things for people too!"

George leaned back in his chair, folding his arms. "Well, that's mighty kind of you all, but I'm not sure if you understand. It's not about doing anything big or fancy. It's just about small acts of kindness, simple things to brighten people's days."

The boy who had first spoken, whose name was Max, nodded seriously. "We know. That's why we think we can help. We've got ideas, too. Fun ideas!"

Martha tilted her head, intrigued. "Ideas? What kind of ideas?"

Max grinned, his confidence growing. "Like, we could use chalk to draw happy pictures on the sidewalks or write nice messages. Or we could hand out balloons in the park. And we can organize games for the younger kids—like tag or hopscotch—so everyone has something fun to do."

One of the other kids, a girl named Emma, added, "We thought maybe we could make paper flowers too, since real ones are expensive. We could decorate the town with them!"

Martha and George listened with growing amazement. What had begun as their quiet, personal mission to spread joy was now blossoming into something much bigger, something they hadn't foreseen. These children, with their boundless energy and fresh ideas, wanted to be part of the movement.

George scratched his chin thoughtfully. "Well, you certainly have a lot of ideas. But this isn't just about having fun. It's about making people feel better, really helping them."

Max nodded eagerly. "We know! And that's why we think we can help. People smile when they see fun things, right? If we make people happy, then it's the same as what you're doing."

Martha, always the more practical one, gave them a cautious look. "It's not that we don't appreciate your enthusiasm, but we need to be sure that you're serious about this. It's easy to get excited about something new, but keeping it going takes effort. Are you all really up for that?"

The kids nodded fervently, a few even bouncing on their toes as if they couldn't wait to get started. "We are! We promise!" Max said.

Martha smiled, her heart softening. She glanced at George, who gave her a small nod. It seemed they were both thinking the same thing. Maybe it was time to let the next generation in.

"Alright," Martha said, her voice kind but firm. "We'll give it a try. But you'll need to remember that this isn't just about having fun for fun's sake. It's about spreading kindness. If you're all serious about that, then welcome to *The Joyful Revolution*."

The kids cheered, their excitement palpable. Max and Emma high-fived, and the younger ones giggled in delight.

"Okay, team," George said, standing up and rubbing his hands together. "What's the plan? You've got your ideas, now let's figure out how we're going to make them happen."

Over the next few days, the children's ideas began to take shape. It was a whirlwind of activity, with Martha and George guiding the kids while also letting them take the lead on their projects. The town square, where the flower giveaway had taken place, became their base of operations.

One of the first projects was the sidewalk chalk drawings. Armed with brightly colored chalk, the kids split into groups and began decorating the town's walkways with cheerful images and positive messages. There were rainbows, smiling suns, and messages like *"You're Awesome!"* and *"Have a Great Day!"* scattered all over the pavement.

George stood back, watching as the kids drew, a grin spreading across his face. "You know, this might actually work."

Martha, sitting on a nearby bench with a cup of tea, nodded. "It's simple, but effective. People are already smiling as they walk by."

Indeed, the reaction from the town was almost immediate. Passersby stopped to admire the chalk art, some taking pictures, while others simply smiled as they read the positive messages. A few parents even stopped to let their younger children join in, adding their own scribbles to the pavement.

Next up were the balloons. Max had come up with the idea to hand out colorful balloons in the park, and the younger kids were especially excited about this plan. Martha and George had initially been skeptical—after all, balloons seemed more suited to children's parties than spreading joy around town—but the kids were adamant.

Armed with a bunch of helium-filled balloons, the group set up in the park on a sunny Saturday afternoon. As families strolled by, the kids would approach with a balloon and a smile, offering it with a simple, "Here, this is for you!"

The response was overwhelmingly positive. Children were delighted by the surprise, tugging their parents toward the balloon station. Even some adults, after an initial moment of hesitation, accepted the balloons with a chuckle, walking away with a bit of cheer in their step.

Martha, watching from a distance, turned to George. "I have to admit, I wasn't sure about the balloons. But look at the smiles."

George nodded. "It's funny how something so small can make such a big difference."

The final project that week was a spontaneous game of tag in the park, organized by Emma and Max. It was a simple idea—no equipment needed, just a wide-open space and a group of kids eager to run around. What started as a game between the kids in *The Joyful Revolution* soon grew into something much bigger as other children in the park joined in. Laughter echoed through the air as the kids ran and played, their joy infectious.

By the end of the afternoon, even George had been roped into the game, much to Martha's amusement.

"You're not as young as you used to be, you know," she teased as he sat down on the grass, catching his breath after a particularly enthusiastic chase.

"Tell me about it," George panted, wiping sweat from his brow. "But hey, it's all for a good cause."

Martha smiled, her heart swelling with pride. She hadn't expected their small revolution to gain such momentum, and certainly not from a group of local kids. But now, seeing the joy that their simple activities had brought to the town, she realized that *The Joyful Revolution* was growing in ways she had never imagined.

As the days went by, more and more children joined in, each bringing their own ideas and enthusiasm to the revolution. Martha and George found themselves at the heart of a multi-generational movement, one that was fueled by kindness, creativity, and a shared desire to make the world just a little bit brighter.

It wasn't about grand gestures or elaborate plans. It wasn't even about flowers or balloons or games. It was about the small, sincere acts of kindness that reminded people of the goodness in the world.

And in the hands of these children, *The Joyful Revolution* had taken on a life of its own.

THE JOYFUL REVOLUTION

One evening, after a long day of chalk drawing, balloon handing, and laughter-filled games, Martha and George sat together on their porch, watching the sun set over the town.

"Who would have thought," George said softly, "that our little idea would inspire all this?"

Martha smiled, leaning her head on his shoulder. "It's like we said before, George. It's not about changing the world overnight. It's about those little moments that remind people they're not alone."

George nodded, his heart full. "And now, we've got a whole new generation carrying it forward."

As the stars began to twinkle overhead, Martha and George knew one thing for certain: The Joyful Revolution was no longer just theirs. It belonged to everyone now.

Chapter 9: Tech Troubles

Martha and George had never imagined that *The Joyful Revolution* would grow the way it had. With the local kids fully on board, their efforts to spread happiness had expanded far beyond their initial dreams. Sidewalks were covered with cheerful chalk drawings, balloons bobbed in the hands of grinning children, and the sound of laughter had become a familiar part of the park. It was everything Martha and George had hoped for, and more.

But then one day, during a meeting of their growing revolution, Max, the unofficial leader of the kids, made a suggestion that caught Martha and George completely off guard.

"You guys should take this online," Max said, grinning as he held up his phone. "You could reach so many more people if you started posting stuff on social media."

Martha blinked at him, her forehead creasing in confusion. "Online? Social media?"

George, who was equally bewildered, leaned forward. "What's social media, lad?"

The kids around them exchanged glances, trying to stifle their giggles. Emma, always helpful, chimed in. "You know, like Facebook, Instagram, or TikTok. You post pictures and videos, and people see them and share them. You'd be famous in no time!"

George scratched his head, still unsure. "Famous, you say? We're not looking for fame, Emma. We just want to make people smile."

Max waved his phone. "Exactly! You'd make *so* many more people smile if you went online. You can post pictures of the chalk drawings, the balloons, all the fun stuff we're doing. People could see it from all over the world!"

THE JOYFUL REVOLUTION

Martha and George exchanged a glance, their faces a mixture of skepticism and curiosity. The idea of taking their little revolution beyond the town was tempting, but this "online" business seemed like a foreign language to them. After all, their idea of cutting-edge technology was the cordless phone they'd bought in 1998.

"Are you sure it's not too complicated?" Martha asked, frowning slightly. "I mean, we're not exactly... tech-savvy."

Max smiled encouragingly. "It's super easy. I can show you! All you have to do is take pictures and post them. It'll be great, I promise."

The next day, Max and a few other kids came over to Martha and George's house, ready to set them up with their first social media accounts. They crowded around the kitchen table, phones and laptops in hand, while Martha and George sat on the other side, looking both excited and nervous.

"So, first things first," Max said, holding up his phone. "We're going to make you a profile on Instagram. It's where you can post pictures and videos of all the cool stuff we're doing. Just think of it like a photo album that the whole world can see."

Martha leaned forward, peering at the phone. "A photo album for the whole world? That sounds... well, a bit strange, doesn't it?"

George, always the practical one, frowned. "Why would anyone want to see our photo album? It's just us and our little revolution."

Max shrugged, still smiling. "Trust me, people *love* this stuff. Kindness and positivity are super popular online."

With that, Max tapped a few buttons and, within moments, Martha and George had their very own Instagram profile. The kids helped them pick a profile picture—an old photo of them from their garden—and then Max handed George the phone.

"Okay, now you're ready to post something," Max said. "All you have to do is take a picture, write a little caption, and hit 'share.' Easy peasy."

George looked down at the phone in his hand, his brow furrowed in concentration. He pointed the camera at Martha, who smiled uncertainly, and pressed the button. The phone made a little click, indicating the photo had been taken.

"There! How's that?" George asked, handing the phone back to Max.

Max looked at the screen, then burst out laughing. "Uh, George, you took a picture of your thumb."

Sure enough, the entire screen was filled with a blurry close-up of George's thumb. Martha snorted, unable to hold back her laughter. Even George chuckled at his mistake.

"Right, right," George said, grinning sheepishly. "Let's try that again."

After a few more attempts—and several more thumb pictures—they finally managed to get a decent shot of Martha sitting in the garden. Max showed them how to write a caption, and after much deliberation, they settled on something simple: *"Spreading joy, one smile at a time."*

With a final tap, the post was live.

"Now what?" George asked, looking at the phone expectantly. "Do we just wait for people to find it?"

Max nodded. "Yep! People will start seeing it and liking it. You might even get some comments."

Sure enough, within minutes, their post received its first few likes. Martha's eyes widened in surprise. "People are already seeing it? That fast?"

Emma nodded. "Yep! That's the power of the internet."

For a moment, it seemed like this whole social media thing might actually work. Martha and George were feeling quite proud of themselves. But then things started to go downhill.

It began with their second post. This time, Martha wanted to post a picture of the kids drawing chalk messages on the sidewalk. She carefully took the photo, making sure to avoid any more thumb-related incidents, and then she and George worked together to come up with a caption.

"How about something like, 'Spreading joy with every step!'" Martha suggested.

George nodded. "That sounds good."

Satisfied, they hit "share," but as soon as they did, a flood of notifications appeared on their screen. Comments began pouring in—only, they weren't the kind of comments Martha and George were expecting.

"Why is your photo upside down?" one person asked.

"Is that supposed to be a picture of feet?" someone else commented.

Confused, Martha and George looked at the photo again. To their dismay, they realized they had somehow posted the picture upside down, and most of what was visible was a random passerby's shoes.

"Ah, for crying out loud," George muttered, shaking his head. "This thing's more trouble than it's worth."

But the troubles didn't stop there. Over the next few days, as Martha and George tried their best to navigate the strange world of social media, things only got more complicated. They accidentally posted a picture of their grocery list instead of their latest chalk drawing. George left a confusing comment on someone else's post, thinking he was replying to their own, and Martha somehow managed to tag the local butcher shop in a photo of balloons.

"We're just trying to spread happiness," Martha muttered one evening, staring at the phone in frustration. "Why does it have to be so complicated?"

As the days passed, the kids tried to help Martha and George with their tech troubles, but it became increasingly clear that social media just wasn't their thing. Every attempt to post something seemed to end in disaster, and their online presence became more of a running joke than a source of inspiration.

Max, ever the optimist, kept encouraging them to stick with it. "You'll get the hang of it eventually," he said one afternoon as he helped them delete yet another accidental post.

But George wasn't so sure. "I don't know, lad. It feels like we're spending more time fixing mistakes than actually spreading joy."

Martha nodded in agreement. "Maybe we're just not cut out for this online business."

The final straw came one evening when Martha accidentally sent a private message to the mayor, thinking she was sending it to George. The message was a string of confused emojis, and to make matters worse, Martha had signed it, *"With love, Martha and George."*

When the mayor replied with a polite but baffled, *"I'm not sure what this means, but thank you?"*, Martha threw her hands up in defeat.

"That's it," she declared. "I'm done. This social media stuff isn't for us."

George, who had been trying to figure out how to delete the message for the past ten minutes, sighed in relief. "Thank goodness. I thought we'd never see the end of this."

That night, as they sat together on their porch, Martha and George reflected on their brief and disastrous foray into the world of social media.

"You know," George said after a long silence, "I think we were right from the start."

"Right about what?" Martha asked.

"About sticking to what we know. This whole social media thing... it's fine for the kids, but it's not for us. We're better off doing things the old-fashioned way—face to face."

Martha nodded thoughtfully. "You're right. We don't need the internet to spread joy. We've been doing just fine without it."

THE JOYFUL REVOLUTION

They sat in comfortable silence for a while, watching the stars twinkle overhead. Despite their tech troubles, they knew they had made the right decision. *The Joyful Revolution* wasn't about likes, comments, or followers—it was about real, human connections. It was about the smiles they saw in the park, the laughter of children drawing on the sidewalk, and the small moments of kindness that brightened someone's day.

In the end, they didn't need the internet to spread happiness. All they needed was each other, and the world right in front of them.

With renewed determination, Martha and George decided that from now on, they would stick to what they knew best—kindness, simplicity, and face-to-face interactions.

As George put it, "We may not be social media influencers, but we sure know how to spread a little joy."

Chapter 10: Pranks with Purpose

The sun was just beginning to rise over the quiet town as Martha poured herself a cup of tea and settled into her favorite chair on the porch. The early morning was her favorite time of day—the peaceful quiet, the gentle breeze, the chirping of birds. It was the perfect moment for reflection. Martha sipped her tea, feeling content and proud of the Joyful Revolution she and George had started.

But as she glanced over at George, who was sitting next to her, a mischievous grin on his face, she had a feeling that something was brewing—something mischievous.

"You're awfully quiet this morning, George," she said, raising an eyebrow. "What's going on in that head of yours?"

George chuckled, his eyes twinkling with mischief. "Oh, I've been thinking, love. We've done a lot of good with our chalk drawings, balloons, and flowers. But maybe it's time to... spice things up a bit."

Martha narrowed her eyes at him, though she couldn't help the smile tugging at her lips. "Spice things up, eh? What exactly are you planning?"

"Just a bit of harmless fun," George replied, leaning back in his chair. "You know, laughter is one of the best ways to spread joy. I think it's time we start playing a few pranks around town—nothing mean, just enough to give people a good chuckle."

Martha groaned, but the glint in her eyes gave her away. She had known George long enough to see where this was headed, and while she was usually the sensible one between the two, even she couldn't deny the appeal of a good-natured prank.

"Pranks, you say? And what exactly do you have in mind?" Martha asked, half-expecting some outrageous scheme.

THE JOYFUL REVOLUTION

"Well," George said, rubbing his hands together as though he'd been waiting for this question, "I've got a few ideas. How about we start small? I was thinking we could swap the sugar packets at the café with salt. Just for a bit of fun—only for a little while, of course."

Martha rolled her eyes, though a smile was already creeping onto her face. "George, you do realize that might cause a bit of chaos, right? People take their coffee very seriously."

George chuckled. "Exactly! But we'll swap them back before anyone gets too grumpy. It'll be like... a test to see if people can laugh at themselves."

Martha sighed, though the corners of her mouth twitched in amusement. "Fine. But if we're going to do this, we need to be clever about it. No one can find out it was us."

George winked. "I wouldn't dream of getting caught."

The next morning, with a basket full of sugar and salt packets, Martha and George made their way to the local café. It was a cozy little spot that the townspeople frequented, especially for their morning coffee and pastries. The café owner, a kind woman named Ellie, greeted them with a cheerful wave as they entered.

"Good morning, Martha, George! What brings you two in so early?" Ellie asked, her hands busy arranging fresh muffins on the counter.

"Oh, just popping in for a cup of tea," Martha said, smiling innocently. "We thought we'd enjoy the morning here for a change."

As Ellie prepared their tea, George slipped over to the condiment station, his heart pounding with excitement. He discreetly swapped out the sugar packets for salt, careful not to draw any attention. Martha stood by, keeping a lookout, her heart racing as well, though she tried to keep her face neutral.

When Ellie brought their tea to the table, George gave Martha a quick wink. The trap was set.

For the next hour, they sat at their table, sipping tea and watching the unsuspecting customers pour salt into their coffee instead of sugar. The reactions were priceless—people would take a sip, then immediately sputter in surprise, staring at their cups in confusion. Some even went back to the counter, thinking something had gone wrong with the coffee itself.

Martha had to bite her lip to keep from laughing out loud. George, meanwhile, was barely containing his amusement, his eyes twinkling with mischief.

"Look at that one," George whispered, pointing to a man who had just tasted his salty coffee and was now frantically adding more milk in an attempt to fix it.

Martha shook her head, but she was laughing too. "We're terrible, George. We're going to get caught."

"Not if we switch them back now," George said with a grin.

Before anyone could figure out what was going on, George quickly swapped the salt packets back with sugar. By the time Ellie wandered over to ask if everything was all right, no one had a clue what had happened.

Martha and George left the café with grins on their faces, knowing that they had caused a few moments of confusion but nothing too serious. The best part was that by the time people figured out their coffee tasted normal again, they were laughing about it.

"One down, plenty more to go," George said as they walked home, already planning their next prank.

The next day, George's mischievous streak continued, this time with an idea involving rubber ducks. "Everyone loves a good rubber duck, right?" he said to Martha as they stood in their living room, a large bag of colorful rubber ducks in hand.

Martha eyed the bag suspiciously. "And what exactly are we going to do with these?"

THE JOYFUL REVOLUTION

"We're going to hide them all over town," George explained, grinning from ear to ear. "People will start finding them in the most unexpected places—on benches, in shop windows, in the park. It'll be like a little scavenger hunt, only they won't know they're playing."

Martha shook her head, but she couldn't suppress the smile on her face. George's ideas were ridiculous, but she had to admit, they always managed to bring a bit of fun to the town. "All right, then. Let's get to work."

For the next few hours, Martha and George wandered around town, discreetly placing rubber ducks in all sorts of nooks and crannies. They hid them in flower pots, on ledges, even in the mailbox of the town hall. By the time they were done, the town was filled with these little yellow surprises.

The reactions were even better than they had hoped. Throughout the day, they watched as people stumbled upon the rubber ducks, their faces lighting up with surprise and amusement. Some people took the ducks home with them, while others left them for someone else to find. It became the talk of the town—no one knew where the ducks were coming from, but everyone was enjoying the mystery.

"Look at that," George said proudly as they watched a group of children giggling as they found a duck perched on a fence. "A bit of harmless fun, and everyone's smiling."

Martha couldn't help but laugh. "You're a menace, George. But I have to admit, this was a good one."

But George wasn't done yet. His next idea involved balloons—lots and lots of balloons.

"We're going to tie balloons to people's cars," George explained one afternoon as they stood in their driveway, surrounded by a mountain of colorful helium balloons.

Martha looked at the balloons, her hands on her hips. "You do realize that people are going to be very confused when they see these on their cars, right?"

"That's the point!" George said, laughing. "It's harmless fun. Imagine walking out of the grocery store and finding your car covered in balloons. You'd have to laugh."

Martha raised an eyebrow but couldn't argue with that logic. "All right, but we're going to have to be quick. We don't want anyone seeing us."

So, armed with a bundle of balloons, Martha and George set off on their next mission. They made their way to the local shopping center, where they discreetly tied balloons to the side mirrors of parked cars. Some cars ended up with just one balloon, while others had entire clusters bobbing in the wind.

By the time they were done, the parking lot looked like a sea of colorful balloons, swaying gently in the breeze.

As people started returning to their cars, the reactions were priceless. Some stared in disbelief, others burst out laughing, and a few even took pictures of their balloon-covered vehicles. One man, after a moment of confusion, started untying the balloons and handing them out to the kids nearby.

Martha and George watched from a distance, grinning like a couple of schoolchildren who had just pulled off the ultimate prank.

"That went better than I expected," Martha admitted as they made their way home. "I thought someone might get annoyed, but everyone seemed to love it."

George beamed with pride. "See? Pranks don't have to be mean to be funny. It's all about bringing a bit of unexpected joy."

Over the next few days, the town was buzzing with talk of the mysterious pranks. No one knew who was behind the rubber ducks, the balloons, or the café salt incident, but that only added to the fun. People started joking about the "Prankster Phantom" and wondering what would happen next.

THE JOYFUL REVOLUTION

For Martha and George, it was the perfect outcome. Their pranks had brought laughter and joy to the town without causing any harm, and that was exactly what they had hoped for.

As they sat together on the porch one evening, watching the sun set over the town, Martha turned to George with a smile. "You know, I wasn't sure about this whole prank thing at first, but I have to admit—it's been a lot of fun."

George chuckled, wrapping his arm around her shoulders. "I knew you'd come around, love. Sometimes, all people need is a little nudge in the right direction—a reminder to laugh at life's little surprises."

Martha leaned her head on his shoulder, feeling a deep sense of contentment. The Joyful Revolution was continuing to spread, and with every small act of kindness, every bit of laughter, they were making a difference.

And as they sat there, watching the last rays of sunlight fade, they both knew that the best was yet to come

Chapter 11: A Growing Movement

Martha and George had always believed that even the smallest acts of kindness could ripple out and touch countless lives. But they hadn't anticipated just how far their Joyful Revolution would spread. What had started with chalk messages, balloons, and a few harmless pranks had quickly grown into something much larger. The town, once quiet and unassuming, was now buzzing with a newfound energy. And the best part? It was contagious.

As Martha sat on the porch one morning, sipping her tea and gazing out at the neighborhood, she noticed something different. The usual hustle and bustle seemed to have softened. There was a calmness to the streets, a quiet but noticeable change in how people moved and interacted. Neighbors greeted each other more warmly, strangers exchanged smiles more often, and there was a lightness in the air that hadn't been there before.

It was subtle at first—just a few more waves from passersby, a couple of extra hellos from people at the grocery store. But soon, Martha and George began to see the real impact of their efforts. The town was transforming, not in a dramatic, showy way, but in a way that was deeply personal to each person living there.

One day, while George was in town running errands, he noticed a group of older gentlemen sitting on a bench, chatting and laughing. He recognized them as some of the town's longtime residents, men who had known each other for decades but rarely seemed to have time to really connect anymore. As he passed by, George couldn't help but smile. It was moments like these—simple and genuine—that made all the difference.

"Morning, gents!" George called out with a wave as he approached them.

THE JOYFUL REVOLUTION 67

"George!" one of the men, Harold, waved back. "Good to see you, old chap. We were just talking about you and Martha, actually."

"Is that so?" George replied, intrigued. He pulled up a seat next to them.

Harold, a kind man with a thick head of white hair, leaned in conspiratorially. "We've been hearing about all the fun you've been stirring up around town. Rubber ducks in flower pots, balloons on cars, and those hilarious chalk drawings. It's all anyone can talk about."

The other men chuckled in agreement, their eyes twinkling with amusement. "The whole town's buzzing with it, George," another man, Arthur, added. "And we were thinking—why should you two have all the fun?"

George's eyebrows shot up. "Oh? What are you lot suggesting?"

Harold grinned. "We want in, of course! We've got a few ideas of our own, you know."

George's heart swelled with pride and excitement. He and Martha had always hoped that their movement would catch on, but they hadn't expected it to grow so quickly—or for it to inspire others in the way it had.

"Well, now, I think that's a splendid idea," George said with a wide grin. "Why don't we meet up later and plan something? The more the merrier, after all."

That evening, George couldn't wait to tell Martha about his conversation with the other seniors in town. As they sat down for dinner, he recounted the story, his excitement practically bubbling over.

"You should've seen them, Martha! They're raring to go. Harold, Arthur, and a few of the others—they've got ideas, too. They want to join the Joyful Revolution."

Martha, ever the cautious one, raised an eyebrow. "And what exactly are their ideas, George? You know how things can get out of hand."

George chuckled. "Oh, nothing too wild. But it's amazing, isn't it? People are starting to realize that joy and connection don't have to be complicated. It's about the little things—the smiles, the laughter, the shared moments."

Martha smiled softly, nodding in agreement. "I never thought it would grow like this. But I'm glad it has. It feels like the town is waking up, doesn't it?"

"It does," George agreed, his eyes twinkling. "And it's only going to get better."

Over the next few weeks, Martha and George found themselves at the center of a rapidly growing movement. More and more people, especially seniors, began reaching out to them, asking how they could get involved. The town's older residents, who had once kept to themselves, were now meeting regularly to discuss new ideas for spreading joy and connecting with others.

The movement had sparked something deeper—a sense of belonging, of purpose. People who had once felt isolated or disconnected from the community were now coming together, finding common ground in their shared mission to bring happiness to those around them.

One afternoon, Martha and George met with a group of seniors at the local park to brainstorm new ways to keep the momentum going. Harold, Arthur, and a few others had arrived early, already deep in discussion when Martha and George arrived.

"Right, so what are we thinking?" George asked as he sat down with the group.

Harold, ever the planner, had a notepad in front of him. "Well, we've been talking, and we think it's time to expand our efforts. We've got the pranks and surprises down pat, but what if we started organizing small gatherings? Like impromptu picnics or game nights in the park?"

Arthur chimed in. "Yeah, nothing too formal—just a way for people to come together, relax, and have a bit of fun. We could even bring some music, maybe a little dancing if anyone's up for it."

Martha listened quietly, her heart swelling with pride. The ideas being shared weren't just about fun—they were about reconnecting, about building a community that valued togetherness over isolation. She glanced at George, who was nodding enthusiastically.

"I love it," Martha finally said, her voice warm with approval. "It's exactly what we've been aiming for—bringing people together in simple ways."

"Exactly," Harold agreed. "It's amazing how much joy you can spread just by being present with each other. People forget that sometimes."

The first of these gatherings took place the following weekend. Martha and George, along with Harold, Arthur, and a few others, set up picnic blankets in the park and invited anyone who wanted to join. They brought along snacks, games, and a small portable speaker for music. Word spread quickly, and by mid-afternoon, the park was filled with laughter and chatter as families, friends, and even strangers came together.

Children played tag and hide-and-seek while their parents lounged on blankets, chatting with neighbors they hadn't spoken to in years. Some of the older residents brought card games, and soon there were clusters of people playing rounds of rummy and bridge, sharing stories and memories.

Martha and George walked around the park, taking it all in. They couldn't believe the transformation they were witnessing. The town, which had once felt so disconnected, was now alive with conversation and connection. People were laughing, sharing stories, and building bonds that had long been neglected.

At one point, George spotted Harold and Arthur leading a group of seniors in a lively game of bocce ball, their faces lit up with joy.

Martha smiled as she watched a group of teenagers help an elderly couple set up their picnic blanket, showing a level of kindness and patience that warmed her heart.

As the sun began to set and the gathering started to wind down, Martha and George found themselves sitting on a bench, watching the last of the families pack up their things. The sense of fulfillment they felt was almost overwhelming.

"It's working, George," Martha said softly, her eyes misty with emotion. "People are coming together again. It's like we've reminded them of something they'd forgotten—that life's joys are meant to be shared."

George nodded, his heart full. "It's amazing, isn't it? And the best part is, it's not about us anymore. It's about everyone. This movement is theirs now, too."

As the weeks passed, the Joyful Revolution continued to grow. The gatherings in the park became a regular occurrence, drawing more and more people each time. Other parts of the town began to follow suit—small acts of joy and connection started popping up everywhere.

At the local grocery store, someone left a basket of fresh flowers at the entrance with a note that read, "Take one and spread the joy." A group of teenagers started organizing spontaneous outdoor concerts, playing music in the town square and encouraging people to dance along. Even the local library got involved, setting up a "Kindness Corner" where people could leave notes of encouragement for others to find.

The town, once so quiet and ordinary, had become a place filled with warmth, laughter, and connection. It wasn't just about the pranks or the gatherings anymore—it was about the way people were reconnecting with each other, rediscovering the simple pleasures of life.

Martha and George watched all of this unfold with a mixture of pride and awe. They had never expected their small acts of kindness to grow into something so big, but they couldn't have been happier with the result.

One evening, as they sat together on the porch, watching the sun set over their beloved town, George turned to Martha with a contented sigh.

"Look at what we've done, love," he said, his voice soft with wonder. "We've started something beautiful."

Martha smiled, resting her head on his shoulder. "We didn't do it alone, George. This town—these people—they were ready for it. They just needed a little reminder."

George nodded, his heart full. "And now that they've remembered, I don't think they'll ever forget again."

As the stars began to twinkle in the sky, Martha and George sat in peaceful silence, knowing that their work had only just begun. The Joyful Revolution had taken root, and with each passing day, it continued to grow, spreading joy, connection, and laughter to every corner of the town.

Chapter 12: Facing Resistance

The Joyful Revolution had become the heart of the town, bringing smiles and laughter to nearly every street corner. For many, it was a much-needed breath of fresh air, a reminder of simpler times when life wasn't so rushed, when neighbors knew each other by name and when happiness wasn't something to chase but something to create right where you were. Martha and George were at the center of it all, the unseen yet unmistakable spark behind the movement that had transformed their once quiet town into a lively, interconnected community.

But as the old saying goes, not everyone loves change. For every person who embraced the spontaneity, the playfulness, and the sense of togetherness, there were a few who saw it as an unnecessary disruption, an intrusion into the routine they valued. And slowly, the murmurs of dissent began to rise.

It started small, with a few grumbles from local businesses. The first complaint came from Mr. Jenkins, the owner of a quaint little bookstore downtown. His shop, which usually had a steady trickle of customers looking for the latest paperback or a cozy spot to read, had been right in the path of one of the flash mobs organized by the kids. One sunny afternoon, as people danced and laughed just outside his windows, Mr. Jenkins stood behind the counter, arms crossed, his face pinched with disapproval.

"I don't understand why they have to do this right here," he muttered to his assistant as he watched the crowd through the window. "It's distracting. People come here for peace and quiet, not for noise and chaos."

His assistant, a young woman who had been swept up by the energy of the movement herself, smiled softly. "I think it's wonderful, don't you? Look at how happy everyone is."

But Mr. Jenkins wasn't convinced. "Maybe so, but it's bad for business. People aren't coming in when there's a crowd outside making a racket."

The next day, Martha and George received a politely worded letter from Mr. Jenkins, asking if they could kindly direct their activities elsewhere, preferably away from his shop. Martha read it with a frown, her brow creased with concern.

"Well, this isn't what we expected," she said, handing the letter to George.

George, ever the optimist, waved it off with a chuckle. "Oh, it's just one person. Don't let it get to you, Martha. Not everyone likes change, especially when it shows up on their doorstep."

But as the days passed, more complaints started to trickle in. A restaurant owner down the street sent a similar note, explaining that the flash mobs and spontaneous picnics were clogging up the sidewalks and deterring customers. Even the local bank manager stopped Martha and George one morning, grumbling about how the balloons tied to people's cars were becoming a "nuisance."

The resistance wasn't confined to the business owners, either. Some residents were starting to feel that the movement had grown too big, too disruptive. One afternoon, as Martha was walking through town, she overheard a couple talking outside the grocery store.

"Have you seen the latest thing they're doing? Chalk drawings all over the sidewalks again," the woman said, shaking her head. "I nearly tripped over one of those kids running around the other day."

"Yeah, it's getting a bit much, isn't it?" her companion replied. "I mean, it's all well and good in theory, but it's starting to feel like we can't even walk down the street without running into one of their 'happy' gatherings."

Martha's heart sank as she hurried past, her mind spinning with doubt. Was this what people thought of their efforts? Were they really causing more trouble than good?

That evening, Martha and George sat on their porch, the weight of the day pressing down on them. For the first time since they'd started the Joyful Revolution, they felt uncertain, unsure if what they were doing was really making the difference they had hoped for.

"Maybe we've gone too far, George," Martha said quietly, her hands folded in her lap. "I never wanted to be a burden to anyone. And now it feels like all we're doing is getting in people's way."

George, who had been unusually quiet, finally spoke up. "I've been thinking the same thing, Martha. I mean, it's one thing to spread joy, but if people are feeling inconvenienced... well, that's not really the point, is it?"

Martha sighed, her heart heavy. "We wanted to make people happy, to remind them of the simple pleasures in life. But what if we're just... annoying them instead?"

They sat in silence for a long moment, both lost in thought. The porch light flickered softly above them, casting a warm glow over the yard. The night was still, save for the occasional chirp of crickets and the distant hum of cars passing by.

Finally, George broke the silence. "You know, Martha, when we started this, we knew not everyone would understand. We knew there'd be people who didn't want to change, people who liked things just the way they were."

Martha nodded, her eyes downcast. "But I didn't think they'd be so against it."

"Neither did I," George admitted. "But then again, maybe that's the point. Change isn't easy, and sometimes it ruffles feathers. But think about all the good we've done. Think about the people who've found joy again, who've reconnected with each other because of what we started."

THE JOYFUL REVOLUTION

Martha looked up at him, her expression softening. "You're right. We've seen so many smiles, so much laughter. It's just... it's hard not to let the negativity get to you, isn't it?"

George nodded. "It is. But if we back down now, what does that say? That we were only in it when it was easy? That we'll stop just because a few people don't like it?"

Martha thought about that for a moment. "I suppose you're right," she said slowly. "We didn't start this to please everyone. We started it because we believed in the power of joy, in the importance of connection. And if that means facing a little resistance along the way... well, maybe that's just part of the journey."

George smiled at her, his eyes twinkling with the same mischief and optimism that had driven them from the start. "Exactly. And who knows? Maybe those who are grumbling now will come around in time. We just have to stay true to what we believe in."

With renewed resolve, Martha and George decided to press on, despite the growing resistance. They began to think carefully about how they could continue spreading joy without causing too much disruption. They still wanted to make people smile, but they also wanted to be considerate of those who found the spontaneity overwhelming.

One evening, they gathered with some of the other seniors involved in the movement to discuss their next steps.

"We've been hearing some complaints," Martha said, addressing the group. "Some people are finding our gatherings and pranks a little... inconvenient."

Arthur, always the jokester, chuckled. "Inconvenient? How can joy be inconvenient?"

"Well," Martha continued, "I think some people are just set in their routines. They're not used to the kind of spontaneous fun we've been having, and it's taking them by surprise."

Harold, ever the practical one, nodded. "I get it. Not everyone likes surprises. But that doesn't mean we should stop. We just need to find a balance."

"Exactly," George said. "We've done so much good already, and we've seen the impact this movement has had. But maybe we need to be a bit more mindful of where and when we hold our gatherings. We don't want to alienate anyone."

The group nodded in agreement, and together they brainstormed new ways to keep the Joyful Revolution alive without causing too much disruption. They decided to move the flash mobs to quieter parts of town, away from the busier streets. The picnics would still happen, but they would make sure to leave space for others who weren't part of the gatherings. And they agreed to tone down some of the pranks, making them less frequent but no less fun.

As the days passed, Martha and George noticed that the tension in town began to ease. While there were still a few who grumbled, the majority of people seemed to appreciate the changes. The gatherings continued, the smiles and laughter persisted, but there was a new sense of harmony. The Joyful Revolution had found its stride once again.

One afternoon, as Martha was walking through town, she passed by Mr. Jenkins' bookstore. She hesitated for a moment, then stepped inside. Mr. Jenkins, who had been rearranging a stack of books, looked up as she approached.

"Ah, Mrs. Willis," he said, his tone neutral. "What can I do for you today?"

Martha smiled gently. "I wanted to apologize, Mr. Jenkins. I know some of our activities have been disruptive to your business, and that was never our intention."

Mr. Jenkins sighed, wiping his hands on a cloth. "I appreciate that, Mrs. Willis. It's just... I run a quiet shop here. The noise and the crowds—well, it's not exactly good for business."

"I understand," Martha said softly. "We've made some changes to be more mindful of that. But I hope you can see that we're just trying to bring a little more joy to the town. It's not about causing trouble. It's about making people smile."

Mr. Jenkins studied her for a moment, then nodded. "I suppose there's something to be said for that. I've noticed people seem... happier lately."

"They are," Martha said. "And that's all we wanted."

Mr. Jenkins gave her a small, reluctant smile. "Well, keep up the good work then. Just maybe... a little quieter next time?"

Martha chuckled. "We'll do our best."

As she left the shop, Martha felt a renewed sense of purpose. There would always be resistance to change, but that didn't mean they were on the wrong path. With each step they took, with every smile they created, the Joyful Revolution continued to grow, weaving its way into the fabric of the town. And Martha and George knew that no matter the obstacles, they would keep going—one joyful act at a time.

Chapter 13: The Setback

The Joyful Revolution had become more than just a movement; it was the heartbeat of the town, pulsing through its streets and touching everyone in some way or another. Martha and George were at the center of it all, the quiet but powerful force behind the wave of happiness that had taken over their little corner of the world. Yet, just as everything seemed to be going so well, a sudden and unexpected setback threatened to unravel it all.

It started one chilly morning, when Martha woke up feeling unusually tired. She had spent the previous day organizing another flash mob and a spontaneous tea party in the park, so at first, she thought it was just exhaustion catching up with her. But as she sat up in bed, a heavy ache spread through her body, and she felt a deep weariness that she couldn't shake. The simple act of getting out of bed felt monumental.

"George," she called out softly, her voice hoarse and weak.

George, who was downstairs brewing their morning tea, immediately noticed the change in her tone. He hurried upstairs, a concerned look on his face as he found Martha sitting on the edge of the bed, pale and drained of her usual energy.

"Martha, what's wrong?" he asked, rushing to her side.

"I'm not sure," she said with a slight frown. "I just don't feel quite right today. Everything hurts, and I'm so tired."

George gently placed a hand on her forehead, checking for a fever. His face tightened with worry when he felt the warmth radiating from her skin.

"You're burning up, love," he said softly. "You need to rest. I'll call the doctor."

Martha nodded weakly, knowing George was right. She wasn't one to complain or admit when she was unwell, but this felt different. Something inside her told her she needed to listen to her body this time.

The doctor arrived later that morning, a kind, elderly man who had known Martha and George for years. He examined her carefully, his expression serious but calm.

"It seems like you've caught a nasty virus, Martha," he said gently. "Nothing too serious, but it's going to knock you off your feet for a while. You'll need plenty of rest and fluids, and no overexerting yourself."

Martha sighed, leaning back against her pillows. "How long do you think it will take for me to feel better?"

"Could be a few days, could be a week or more," the doctor replied. "It depends on how well you rest and recover."

George, who had been standing nearby, frowned deeply. "A week? But she's always on her feet, doctor. What about the Revolution? We've got gatherings planned, and—"

"Martha's health comes first, George," the doctor interrupted kindly but firmly. "She's done a lot for this town, but now it's time to let others take care of her. The Joyful Revolution will have to pause for a little while."

Martha opened her mouth to protest, but the doctor raised a hand to stop her.

"No arguments, Martha. If you push yourself now, you'll only make things worse. Trust me, the town will manage for a little while without you."

As the doctor left, George sat by Martha's bedside, holding her hand. The house felt eerily quiet, the usual hum of activity replaced by an unsettling stillness. For the first time in months, they weren't planning the next joyful event or gathering ideas for their next playful prank. The absence of their usual routine weighed heavily on both of them.

"You heard the doctor," George said softly. "You need to rest, Martha. I'll take care of everything."

Martha smiled weakly, though her eyes were filled with frustration. "I know you will, George. But what about the Revolution? The town depends on us to keep things going."

George squeezed her hand. "They'll manage. The others can handle things for a while. You just focus on getting better."

Despite his words, George couldn't help but feel a deep unease settle in his chest. The Joyful Revolution had been their shared mission, a project that had given them both a new sense of purpose. Without Martha by his side, he wasn't sure how to keep it going. The thought of trying to lead the movement on his own felt overwhelming, and as the days passed, he found himself slipping into a quiet sense of loneliness.

The town, too, began to notice the absence of Martha's joyful energy. Without her laughter and enthusiasm, the daily gatherings became less frequent, and the spontaneous events lost some of their spark. People still smiled and greeted each other in the streets, but there was a palpable difference. It was as if a vital part of the movement had gone missing.

George tried his best to keep things going, but it wasn't the same. He missed Martha's steady hand, her gentle encouragement, and her knack for turning even the smallest of moments into something magical. Without her, everything felt a little duller, a little less vibrant.

The daily meetings that had once been filled with laughter and ideas now felt quieter, more subdued. George would sit at the head of the table, surrounded by the other seniors who had become part of their movement, but his heart wasn't fully in it. He found himself distracted, his mind always wandering back to Martha's bedside and her absence weighing heavily on him.

One afternoon, as they sat around the table discussing their next event, George suddenly stood up, his face etched with frustration.

"I can't do this," he said, his voice strained. "I can't keep this going without her."

The others looked at him in surprise, their expressions filled with concern.

"George, we understand this is hard," said Emily, one of their closest friends. "But Martha would want us to keep going. She's always said this is about more than just the two of you."

George shook his head, his hands clenched into fists. "I know she would, but it doesn't feel right. Everything we've done, we've done together. How can I keep this up when she's not by my side?"

There was a long pause as the group exchanged glances, unsure of what to say. Finally, Arthur spoke up, his voice gentle but firm.

"George, we all care about this movement just as much as you do. And we care about you and Martha. But you're not alone in this. We're all here to help. You don't have to carry the weight of this by yourself."

George sat back down, his shoulders slumping with the weight of his emotions. "I just don't know if I'm strong enough to do it without her."

That evening, after the meeting had ended, George made his way back home, his heart heavy with doubt. He had always been the optimistic one, the one who believed in the power of joy and laughter to change lives. But without Martha, he felt lost. Their mission had given him purpose, but now that she was ill, he wasn't sure how to carry on.

When he arrived home, he found Martha sitting up in bed, looking a little stronger than she had in the past few days. Her color had returned, and though she was still weak, there was a spark of determination in her eyes.

"How was the meeting?" she asked, her voice still soft but filled with curiosity.

George sat down beside her, letting out a deep sigh. "It wasn't the same without you, Martha. I feel like I'm letting everyone down."

Martha reached out and took his hand, squeezing it gently. "George, you're not letting anyone down. You're doing your best, and that's all anyone can ask of you."

"But it doesn't feel like enough," George said, his voice cracking with emotion. "I don't know how to keep this going without you."

Martha smiled softly, her eyes filled with love and understanding. "You don't have to do it alone, George. The others are there to help. And this movement isn't just about us—it's about the entire town. We've started something that has taken on a life of its own. Even if I can't be there physically, my spirit is with you every step of the way."

George looked at her, his heart swelling with gratitude and love. "But what if I can't do it without you? What if I don't have the strength?"

Martha's smile grew wider, and she reached up to gently touch his cheek. "You've always had the strength, George. You just need to believe in yourself as much as I believe in you."

Tears filled George's eyes as he leaned down to kiss her forehead. "I don't know what I'd do without you, Martha."

"You'll never have to find out," she whispered, her voice filled with quiet assurance. "We're in this together, no matter what."

As the days passed, George slowly found his way back to the Joyful Revolution, buoyed by Martha's encouragement and the support of their friends. He still felt her absence keenly, but he realized that the movement they had started was bigger than both of them. It was about the community they had built, the joy they had spread, and the sense of connection they had fostered.

The town, too, began to rally around them. People brought meals and flowers to their home, offering their well wishes for Martha's recovery. The gatherings continued, though quieter and more thoughtful, as the townspeople realized that the Joyful Revolution was not just about pranks and flash mobs—it was about caring for one another, even in difficult times.

And as George visited Martha each day, sitting by her bedside and sharing stories of the town's continued joy, he began to see that their mission had never been about them alone. It was about the spirit of kindness and connection they had sparked, a spirit that would carry on, no matter the setbacks.

By the end of the week, Martha's health began to improve. The fever broke, and her strength slowly returned. George's loneliness eased as he realized that the Joyful Revolution was still very much alive, even without their daily presence.

Martha, though still recovering, beamed with pride as George shared stories of the town's resilience. Together, they reflected on how far they had come, knowing that no matter what challenges lay ahead, they would face them together—with joy in their hearts and laughter as their guide.

Chapter 14: A Surprise Revival

The days had grown warmer, and the gentle breeze of early spring rustled through the trees, carrying with it the subtle fragrance of blooming flowers. Martha sat propped up in her bed, the soft light filtering through her window. Her recovery was slow but steady, and every day she felt a little stronger. George had become her constant companion, bringing her updates from the Joyful Revolution as it continued, albeit quieter and more subdued, without her active participation.

Yet, despite her improving health, there was a restlessness in her spirit. She missed being part of the movement, missed the spontaneous laughter, the surprise gatherings, and the joy that had become part of their daily lives. George had been wonderful, sharing stories from the town and the kindness of neighbors who brought over meals and flowers, but it wasn't the same. She longed to be out there again, side by side with George, spreading joy.

As the days passed, she could see through her window how the town had shifted. What had started as her and George's playful rebellion against the mundanity of life had become something larger, something that belonged to the whole community. She would watch as children skipped down the streets, singing songs they had made up, or elderly couples who hadn't spoken to each other in years now shared park benches and conversation. Even from her room, she could feel the ripple effects of what they had started.

But there was still something missing—a sense of anticipation, a spark that had been there before. She could tell George was worried about her, and while the town had rallied to keep things going, it lacked the spontaneous bursts of joy they had once shared. Martha wondered whether the Joyful Revolution had lost its momentum. She

THE JOYFUL REVOLUTION

feared that without her and George's constant leadership, the spirit of the movement might fade, leaving only a faint memory of what had once been.

What Martha didn't know was that something was happening beneath the surface, something that would reignite the joy she thought might be slipping away. The children of the town, who had always been the heart of the movement's playful energy, had been quietly planning a surprise. Led by young Amelia, the girl who had once hesitated to join the group but had since become its most spirited member, the children had devised a way to honor Martha and George in a way that would lift the entire town's spirits—and, they hoped, bring a smile back to Martha's face.

One afternoon, as the children gathered in the park for an impromptu game of hopscotch, Amelia brought everyone together in a huddle, her eyes gleaming with excitement.

"I've got an idea," she said, her voice barely containing her enthusiasm. "We need to do something special for Martha and George. Something big. Something that shows them how much they've meant to us and this whole town."

The other children nodded eagerly, curious about what she had in mind.

"What do you mean?" asked Tommy, one of the younger boys. "Like a party?"

"Bigger than a party," Amelia replied, her voice growing more serious. "I'm talking about a parade. A huge, town-wide parade. With balloons, music, and everyone coming together. We can show them that even though Martha's been sick, the Joyful Revolution is still alive—and we're all part of it."

The children gasped in excitement, their eyes lighting up as they imagined the spectacle. A parade! It was perfect. They knew that Martha loved watching the town come alive with joy, and a parade would be the ultimate display of their gratitude and love for her and George.

Over the next few days, the children, with the help of a few parents and other community members, set their plan into motion. They wanted to keep it a secret from Martha and George, so they worked quietly, spreading the word to the rest of the town in whispers and secret meetings. People volunteered their time and resources—sewing banners, making colorful paper decorations, and organizing musicians from the local band to play lively tunes during the parade.

The energy in the town began to shift again, this time with a sense of anticipation that grew with each passing day. People were excited, not only to celebrate Martha and George but to remind themselves of the joy they had rediscovered through the Joyful Revolution. Even local businesses, which had once grumbled about the "disruptive" flash mobs and spontaneous picnics, offered their support, donating supplies and food for the event.

Amelia took on the role of leader, coordinating with the adults and making sure everything was perfect. She was determined that the parade would be a surprise, something that Martha and George could witness from their home without any prior warning.

"We'll march right down their street," Amelia explained to the group during one of their secret planning sessions. "Martha can watch from her window. We'll have balloons, music, dancing, and everything. It's going to be amazing."

The children and adults alike could hardly contain their excitement as the day of the parade drew closer. They rehearsed their songs and dances in small groups, made final preparations for the floats and banners, and ensured that everyone in the town knew where to meet and when to join the procession.

Finally, the day arrived. It was a bright, sunny morning, with a crisp breeze that seemed to carry the spirit of the Joyful Revolution in its wake. The entire town had gathered in secret near the park, just a short distance from Martha and George's home. There was an electric sense of excitement in the air as people donned colorful costumes, painted their faces with cheerful designs, and tied balloons to makeshift floats.

Amelia stood at the front of the procession, a large banner in her hands that read: *"Thank You, Martha and George—For Bringing Joy Back to Our Town!"* She beamed with pride as she looked around at the crowd, filled with both children and adults who had come together for this special moment.

"All right, everyone," she called out, her voice ringing with excitement. "It's time to show Martha and George just how much they mean to us!"

With that, the parade began. The children led the way, skipping and dancing down the street, waving their homemade banners and cheering loudly. Behind them, musicians played upbeat tunes on trumpets and drums, filling the air with music that echoed through the town. Colorful floats, decorated with flowers and streamers, followed, each one more vibrant and joyful than the last.

The townspeople lined the streets, clapping and cheering as the parade passed by. People who hadn't participated in the Joyful Revolution before now found themselves caught up in the excitement, joining in the celebration with smiles and laughter. It was as though the entire town had been waiting for this moment—a chance to come together and celebrate the joy that had quietly taken root in their lives.

Inside her home, Martha had no idea what was happening outside. She had been resting, still recovering from her illness, when she heard the faint sound of music drifting through the window. At first, she thought it was just another gathering in the park, but as the sound grew louder, she realized something bigger was happening.

"George," she called out, her voice filled with curiosity. "Do you hear that?"

George, who had been sitting in the living room, glanced up from his newspaper. He hadn't noticed the music at first, but now that

Martha mentioned it, he could hear it too—lively, joyful music that seemed to be getting closer.

He stood up and walked over to the window, pulling back the curtain. What he saw took his breath away.

"Martha," he said, his voice filled with awe. "You need to see this."

With George's help, Martha slowly made her way to the window. As she looked outside, her eyes widened in disbelief. There, marching down the street, was the most beautiful sight she had ever seen—a parade in full swing, with balloons, banners, music, and smiling faces as far as the eye could see.

She spotted Amelia at the front of the procession, proudly holding the banner that bore her and George's names. Tears welled up in Martha's eyes as she realized what was happening. This parade—this joyous celebration—was for them.

"Oh, George," she whispered, her voice thick with emotion. "Look at what they've done."

George smiled, wrapping his arm around her shoulders. "It's incredible," he said softly. "I think they're trying to tell us something."

As the parade reached their house, the crowd gathered outside, waving and cheering up at Martha and George. The musicians played a lively tune, and the children danced and laughed, their faces glowing with excitement.

Amelia stepped forward, waving up at Martha and George with a wide grin on her face.

"This is for you!" she called out. "Thank you for everything you've done!"

Martha's heart swelled with pride and gratitude. She waved back, tears streaming down her cheeks. For the first time since she had fallen ill, she felt truly alive again—filled with a sense of purpose and connection that she had thought she might never feel again.

As the parade continued, more and more people joined in, until the entire town seemed to be part of the celebration. It wasn't just about

Martha and George anymore—it was about the community they had built together. The Joyful Revolution had taken on a life of its own, and it was clear that it would continue, with or without their constant presence.

Martha and George watched from their window, their hearts full of love and pride for the town they had come to cherish so deeply. The parade was more than just a thank-you—it was a reminder that joy and connection were contagious, and that even in the face of adversity, the spirit of the Joyful Revolution would carry on.

As the final float passed by, and the parade began to wind down, George turned to Martha, his eyes shining with emotion.

"I think we've done something special here," he said quietly.

Martha nodded, her hand resting gently on his arm. "We have," she agreed. "And it's only just beginning."

They stood together in silence for a moment, watching as the parade faded into the distance. The joy they had sparked had grown beyond anything they could have imagined, and now it belonged to everyone.

The Joyful Revolution had become more than just a movement—it was a way of life, and it would continue to bring people together, spreading happiness and connection wherever it went.

Martha smiled, her heart full of hope for the future.

The town had embraced joy—and it was here to stay.

Chapter 15: The Final Plan

The parade had done more than lift Martha's spirits—it had reignited the spark that had been at the heart of the Joyful Revolution. As she sat with George in the days that followed, watching the town continue to buzz with excitement, they realized something profound: they had planted a seed of joy that was now growing in ways they could never have predicted. The people of the town had embraced the movement, and in doing so, they had found happiness not just in the activities but in each other.

But Martha and George knew there was still more they could do. Their mission wasn't complete yet. While the town had certainly felt the effects of the Joyful Revolution, the ripples needed to spread wider. It was time to dream bigger—time to create something that would leave a lasting mark not only on the town but perhaps even beyond.

One evening, as the sun set in shades of pink and orange, Martha turned to George with a mischievous smile playing on her lips.

"I've got an idea," she said, her eyes twinkling with the same energy that had sparked the revolution months ago.

George raised an eyebrow, intrigued by the familiar tone of excitement in her voice. "Oh? Do tell."

Martha leaned in closer. "What if we took everything we've done so far—all the joy, all the connection, all the fun—and made it even bigger? What if we had a city-wide festival? Not just a parade or a flash mob, but a full-blown *Happiness Festival*?"

George's eyes widened as the idea sank in. "A festival... celebrating joy?"

"Exactly!" Martha said, sitting up straighter. "We could bring everyone together for a day of games, music, food, and storytelling. We could invite people from neighboring towns too. This could be the culmination of everything we've worked for—the grandest celebration of joy and community that we've ever seen."

George was quiet for a moment, absorbing the scope of Martha's idea. It was bold, even ambitious. But then again, every great thing they had done so far had started with an ambitious idea. And if anyone could pull off something as grand as a Happiness Festival, it was the two of them—and their incredible town.

"I love it," George finally said, his smile spreading across his face. "But it's going to take a lot of planning."

Martha grinned, already thinking about the possibilities. "That's the fun part. We've got the whole town behind us. The kids, the seniors, everyone. This will be something we all do together."

The next morning, Martha and George gathered the core group of their revolution—the children, the seniors, and a few of the town's most enthusiastic supporters—at the park. The buzz of excitement was palpable as the group settled in, eager to hear what Martha and George had in mind.

Amelia, who had become a key leader of the younger members, was the first to speak. "What's the plan? I can tell you two have something big up your sleeves!"

Martha smiled warmly at Amelia, grateful for her boundless energy and optimism. "We do have something big planned," she said, her voice carrying a note of anticipation. "We're thinking of putting together a city-wide festival—one that celebrates everything we've worked for. A *Happiness Festival*, filled with games, music, food, and storytelling. A day where the entire town, and maybe even people from outside the town, can come together and celebrate joy."

The group erupted in excited chatter. The idea of a festival filled with laughter, music, and fun was exactly what everyone needed. It was a way to celebrate all they had accomplished and to spread their message of happiness even further.

"How are we going to do it?" asked Tommy, one of the younger boys. "There's so much to plan!"

"We'll need everyone's help," George said, his voice steady and calm as he addressed the group. "We'll need to organize teams for different parts of the festival. Games, food, music, decorations—it's going to take all of us working together to make it happen."

Amelia's hand shot up again. "I can help with the games! We'll need fun activities for the kids and the adults!"

"And I can help with food!" Mrs. Jenkins, one of the seniors, chimed in. "We can have a potluck, with everyone bringing their favorite dishes to share."

Others began offering suggestions, their enthusiasm building with each new idea. There would be live music, with local bands and musicians taking turns playing throughout the day. Storytelling circles would be set up, where people of all ages could share their favorite stories, both personal and traditional. There would be art stations, where kids could paint and draw, and photo booths with props for people to take silly pictures with their friends.

The festival began to take shape, piece by piece, as the group brainstormed and assigned tasks. The children were especially excited about the games, coming up with ideas for sack races, scavenger hunts, and tug-of-war competitions. Amelia was put in charge of organizing the children's activities, and she took her new responsibility very seriously, already scribbling down ideas in her notebook.

Meanwhile, the seniors took charge of the food, with Mrs. Jenkins leading the charge to coordinate the potluck. They planned to set up tables in the town square, where everyone could come and sample the homemade dishes that people had prepared. George suggested setting up a barbecue pit as well, and a few of the local restaurants offered to donate food for the event.

The town's musicians also stepped up, offering to perform for free. George, with his knack for organization, put together a schedule so that there would be music throughout the day, with different genres to keep things lively and varied. From folk songs to upbeat pop tunes, the festival would have something for everyone.

As for decorations, the children and the seniors agreed to work together to create colorful banners, streamers, and balloons to fill the streets. They wanted the town to look as festive as possible, so that anyone who arrived would instantly feel the joy in the air.

Over the following weeks, the town came alive with activity. Every day, groups of people met to discuss the festival, finalize plans, and work on their respective tasks. It was as though the entire town had been given a renewed sense of purpose, and the excitement for the upcoming festival was contagious. Even people who hadn't been directly involved in the Joyful Revolution up to this point found themselves swept up in the preparations, eager to contribute in whatever way they could.

The local hardware store donated supplies for building stages and booths, while the florist offered to provide fresh flowers to decorate the town square. Businesses that had once been skeptical of the Joyful Revolution now threw their support behind the festival, recognizing the positive impact it had had on the community.

Martha and George worked tirelessly alongside everyone else, coordinating the various teams and making sure everything was on track. They attended every planning meeting, offering guidance and encouragement but always allowing the townspeople to take ownership of the event. This was, after all, a celebration for everyone.

As the day of the festival approached, excitement reached a fever pitch. The children had finished painting their banners, which now hung proudly along the streets, declaring in bright letters: *"Welcome to the Happiness Festival!"* The musicians had rehearsed their sets, and the food committee had finalized the menu, with dishes ranging from homemade pies to spicy barbecue ribs.

On the morning of the festival, the sun rose over the town, casting a golden glow on the streets. Martha and George stood together in the town square, watching as the final preparations were made. Booths were being set up, musicians were tuning their instruments, and the air was filled with the delicious smells of food being cooked.

"It's really happening," Martha said softly, her eyes glistening with pride and emotion. "We've done it."

George smiled and squeezed her hand. "We haven't done it alone. This town has come together in ways I never imagined. Look at them all."

Martha glanced around, taking in the sight of families setting up picnic blankets, children running through the streets with balloons, and neighbors chatting happily as they helped each other prepare for the day. It was a scene of pure joy, and it filled her heart with a sense of fulfillment that she hadn't realized she had been missing.

The festival officially kicked off at noon, with a grand opening ceremony led by Amelia and Mrs. Jenkins. Amelia, standing proudly on the makeshift stage, welcomed everyone with a bright smile.

"Thank you all for being here," she said, her voice full of excitement. "This festival is a celebration of everything we've done together—of the joy we've found in each other and in our town. So let's have fun, play games, eat delicious food, and most importantly, let's spread happiness!"

The crowd erupted into cheers, and with that, the festival was underway. The children raced to the game stations, where they participated in sack races, egg-and-spoon relays, and tug-of-war contests. Laughter echoed through the streets as adults joined in, their competitive spirits coming alive as they tried to keep up with the kids.

At the same time, the storytelling circles began, with people of all ages gathering to share their favorite tales. Some told personal stories about their own experiences in the town, while others recounted traditional folktales passed down through generations. It was a beautiful reminder of the power of storytelling to connect people, and as the day went on, the circles continued to grow.

Music filled the air, with local bands and musicians taking turns on the stage, playing everything from folk tunes to rock anthems. People danced in the streets, their faces lit up with joy as they moved to the rhythm of the music. Even the shyest members of the community found themselves joining in, swept up in the infectious energy of the festival.

As the sun began to set, casting a warm orange glow over the town, Martha and George stood together once again, this time on the stage. The festival had been an overwhelming success, and as they looked out at the crowd—at the smiles, the laughter, the togetherness—they knew they had accomplished something truly special.

"Thank you," George said, his voice carrying over the crowd. "Thank you for being a part of this journey. We started with a simple idea—to bring joy to our town—but it's become so much more. We've seen the power of happiness, of connection, and of community. And today, we celebrate that."

Martha stepped forward, her voice soft but strong. "This festival is just the beginning. The joy we've created here doesn't end when the day is over. It's something we carry with us, something we can continue to share with each other and with the world. So let's keep spreading happiness, wherever we go."

The crowd erupted into applause, and as Martha and George stepped down from the stage, they were surrounded by friends and neighbors, each one offering words of gratitude and love.

The Happiness Festival had been more than just a celebration—it had been a reaffirmation of everything they had worked for. And as Martha and George stood in the fading light, they knew that the Joyful Revolution had truly succeeded. Joy had taken root in the town, and it would continue to grow for years to come.

The festival had been a triumph, but more than that, it had shown Martha and George just how powerful their mission had become. The people of the town had embraced joy, and they had made it their own.

Chapter 16: The Happiness Festival

The morning of the Happiness Festival dawned with a soft golden light filtering through the trees, casting a warm glow on the town square. It was a perfect day—clear skies and a gentle breeze, as if the weather itself was celebrating alongside the town. Martha and George stood hand in hand, looking out at the transformation before them. Banners and streamers fluttered in the wind, colorful balloons bobbed along the streets, and the faint hum of excitement filled the air as people began to gather.

The weeks of planning had all led to this moment. The hard work, the late nights, and the endless brainstorming had finally paid off. But now that the day had arrived, Martha found herself feeling something she hadn't expected: nervousness. She glanced at George, who gave her hand a reassuring squeeze.

"Are you ready for this?" he asked, his voice steady and calm.

Martha smiled, though her heart was racing. "I think so. I just want everything to go smoothly."

George chuckled softly. "It already has. Look at the town, Martha. This is more than we ever could have imagined."

Martha looked around, and as she did, her worries began to melt away. The streets were filling with people—families, children, seniors—all coming together with smiles on their faces. The air was filled with the smell of fresh food cooking, and the distant sound of laughter could be heard from where the children were setting up their games. It was everything they had hoped for and more.

"We did it," Martha whispered, more to herself than to George.

George grinned. "We sure did."

As the morning unfolded, the festival began in earnest. People of all ages were milling about, exploring the various booths and stations that had been set up throughout the town. There was a sense of anticipation in the air, as though everyone knew this day would be special—one that would be remembered for years to come.

The children's games kicked off first, with Amelia leading the charge. She had put together a series of activities that were simple but fun—sack races, tug-of-war contests, and a scavenger hunt that had the kids running through the streets with excitement. The laughter of children filled the square, and their joy was infectious. Parents stood by, cheering on their kids and even joining in on some of the games, their playful spirits coming alive.

Tommy, one of the younger boys, was racing in the sack race when he tripped and tumbled onto the grass. Instead of tears, however, he burst into laughter, rolling around as the other children followed suit. Soon, a group of kids were laughing uncontrollably, their energy sparking even more joy among the crowd.

Amelia, ever the leader, helped Tommy back to his feet, giving him a high-five. "You did great!" she said with a grin. "Let's see if you can win the next one!"

The sense of camaraderie among the children was heartwarming, and it didn't take long for the adults to get involved as well. The tug-of-war contest, which had originally been set up for the kids, quickly turned into a competition between the younger adults and the older generations. Laughter echoed through the square as the seniors pulled with surprising strength, giving the younger team a run for their money.

Across the square, the music stage had come to life. Local musicians were taking turns performing, filling the air with a mix of folk songs, upbeat tunes, and even a few pop songs that had people dancing in the streets. A group of teenagers had gathered in front of the stage, dancing and singing along to the music, while older couples swayed gently to the rhythm.

THE JOYFUL REVOLUTION

One of the highlights of the festival was a surprise performance by George and a few of the local seniors, who had formed a makeshift band. They took to the stage with a collection of guitars, tambourines, and even a harmonica. The crowd cheered as George, with his usual laid-back demeanor, strummed the opening chords to a lively folk song.

The song was an old favorite, one that everyone in town seemed to know by heart. As George and the others played, the crowd joined in, their voices rising together in a joyful chorus. Martha stood at the edge of the stage, her heart swelling with pride as she watched George perform, his smile as wide as she'd ever seen it.

The music continued throughout the day, with different groups taking the stage to perform. There were moments of high energy, with fast-paced songs that had people clapping and dancing, and quieter moments where the music slowed, allowing people to sit back and simply enjoy the sounds of the festival.

Meanwhile, the potluck tables had been set up near the park, and the food committee had outdone themselves. Long tables were laden with homemade dishes, from pies and casseroles to fresh salads and barbecued meats. The smell of the food wafted through the air, drawing people in from every corner of the festival.

Mrs. Jenkins, who had taken charge of the food station, was bustling around, making sure everything was running smoothly. She greeted each person who came to the table with a smile, offering them a plate and encouraging them to try as many dishes as they could.

"You've got to try my apple pie," she told one young family, her eyes twinkling with pride. "It's my secret recipe."

The family eagerly accepted slices of pie, and soon enough, word had spread about Mrs. Jenkins' famous dessert. People lined up to get a taste, and each one left with a satisfied smile on their face.

Martha and George made their way to the potluck table as well, greeted warmly by everyone they passed. It was clear that the festival had brought out the best in the town—the sense of community, the willingness to share, and the simple pleasure of coming together over a meal.

They filled their plates with food and found a spot near the park, where they could sit and watch the festival unfold. As they ate, they took in the scene before them: children laughing as they played, families sitting together, sharing food and stories, and groups of friends chatting and dancing in the streets.

"This is it, George," Martha said softly, her eyes welling up with emotion. "This is what we dreamed of."

George nodded, his own voice thick with pride. "It's more than we could have ever imagined."

As the afternoon wore on, the festival only seemed to gain more momentum. The sun, now high in the sky, cast a soft glow over the town, and it was as if the whole world had slowed down to join in the celebration. People who hadn't seen each other in years were reconnecting, sharing stories, and reminiscing about old times. The town that had once felt distant and disconnected was now buzzing with laughter, conversation, and joy.

Martha and George, though tired from the day's excitement, couldn't stop smiling. Every corner of the town was alive with the spirit of togetherness. George, ever the observer, pointed out the little details—the spontaneous games of catch between strangers, the way people shared food from their picnic baskets without hesitation, the music that drifted through the air, keeping the mood light and festive.

"I never thought we'd see this," George mused as he watched a group of teenagers tie balloons to a lamppost, laughing as they worked together. "It's like the whole town has come alive again."

Martha nodded, her heart full. "It feels like we've given them a reason to come together. Not just for today, but for the future too."

As they sat there, enjoying the scene, several familiar faces stopped by to greet them. Mrs. Jenkins, the one who'd made the famous apple pie, handed them each another slice with a wink. "You two deserve it," she said, her voice warm with gratitude. "I don't know what we would have done without you."

A group of children ran up next, led by Amelia. They were holding hands and skipping along, their faces bright with excitement. "Martha! George!" Amelia called out as they approached. "We've made something for you!"

Before Martha and George could respond, the children proudly presented them with a large handmade banner. It was covered in colorful drawings, handprints, and scribbled notes of thanks. In bold letters, it read: "Thank you for bringing us joy!"

Martha gasped, her hand flying to her heart. George, equally touched, could only manage a soft, "Wow."

"We wanted to say thank you," Amelia explained with a shy smile. "For everything you've done."

Martha blinked back tears. "Oh, my dears, you didn't have to do this."

"We wanted to," Amelia insisted. "Because you've made this town so much happier."

George chuckled, ruffling the young girl's hair. "I think it's you kids who've made the biggest difference."

The children beamed at the compliment, their faces glowing with pride. They ran off to continue their fun, leaving Martha and George holding the banner, which they draped over the back of their picnic bench.

As the day began to wind down, a special event was announced. The children, always full of surprises, had organized a storytelling circle. At the center of the square, they arranged chairs and blankets in a large circle, inviting everyone to join. The idea was simple: anyone could step forward and share a story, whether it was a personal memory, a funny tale, or something inspiring.

One by one, people began to gather around. The circle filled quickly, with children sitting cross-legged on the blankets and adults finding seats nearby. There was a palpable sense of anticipation in the air, as if everyone knew that this would be a fitting end to the day.

Amelia stood up to introduce the event, her voice bright and clear. "We thought it would be fun to hear some stories," she said. "Stories about happiness, about friendship, or anything that makes us smile."

The first person to step forward was Mr. Willis, the notoriously grumpy neighbor who had once been so resistant to change. He shuffled to the center of the circle, looking a little unsure of himself. Martha and George exchanged surprised glances—Mr. Willis had never been one to participate in town events.

Clearing his throat, Mr. Willis began to speak. "I suppose most of you know me as a bit of a grouch," he said, his voice gruff but steady. "And, well, you wouldn't be wrong. I've spent a lot of years being angry about things that didn't matter much in the grand scheme of things. But something changed when Martha and George came around, spreading their... what do you call it? Joyful Revolution."

The crowd chuckled softly, but Mr. Willis didn't lose his focus.

"I didn't want to be a part of it at first," he continued, rubbing the back of his neck. "I thought it was silly. But, seeing all of you here today, and seeing the way this town has come together... well, I guess I was wrong. I've learned that it's never too late to start seeing the good in things."

The crowd clapped, touched by his honesty. Mr. Willis gave a small, sheepish smile before returning to his seat.

Next up was Mrs. Jenkins, who shared a funny story about her first attempt at baking, much to the delight of the crowd. More people followed, sharing their favorite memories, funny anecdotes, and heartwarming tales. Laughter echoed through the square, punctuated by moments of quiet reflection as people spoke from the heart.

Martha and George sat back, listening with full hearts. It was exactly what they had hoped for—a moment of unity, where the simple act of storytelling could bring people together in a way that nothing else could.

As the sun began to set, casting a soft orange glow over the town, the festival drew to a close. The energy had shifted from the excitement of the day to a quieter, more peaceful contentment. People lingered, reluctant to leave the warmth and connection they had found. The town square, now littered with confetti and balloons, was a testament to the success of the day.

Martha and George stood at the center of it all, watching as people slowly made their way home, still chatting and laughing as they walked. It was a sight they would never forget.

George turned to Martha, his eyes twinkling. "Well, what do you think, love? Did we pull it off?"

Martha smiled, leaning into his embrace. "I think we did more than pull it off. We made something truly special."

As they stood there, soaking in the last moments of the day, Amelia ran up to them once again, breathless and excited.

"Martha! George!" she called out. "We have one last surprise!"

Before they could ask what she meant, the crowd that had gathered earlier for the storytelling circle suddenly erupted into applause. The children, led by Amelia, held up sparklers that lit up the fading sky, creating a magical scene of twinkling lights. It was the perfect end to a perfect day.

Tears filled Martha's eyes as she watched the sparklers glow against the darkening sky. "Look at them, George," she whispered. "They're so full of joy."

George nodded, his heart full. "And so are we."

With that, the Happiness Festival came to a close, leaving behind a town that had been forever changed. What had started as a small idea—two people's desire to spread a little happiness—had blossomed into something far bigger than they could have ever imagined. The Joyful Revolution had taken root, and the town was all the better for it.

As Martha and George made their way home, hand in hand, they knew that this was only the beginning. The joy they had sparked would continue to grow, lighting up their town and, perhaps, beyond. And as they walked through the quiet streets, they couldn't help but smile, knowing that their mission had been a success.

Chapter 17: A World of Joy

As the last remnants of the Happiness Festival faded away, Martha and George found themselves back at their favorite spot—an old, weathered park bench under the shade of a grand oak tree. This bench, nestled in the heart of the town's park, had been their quiet retreat for years. It was here where they'd first dreamed up their mission, where they'd shared countless ideas, laughed about their blunders, and, most importantly, reflected on their small town's transformations.

Now, as they sat side by side, the echoes of laughter from the festival still lingered in the air, and the soft glow of lanterns flickered in the distance. The park was quiet again, save for the occasional chirping of crickets and the gentle rustle of the leaves in the breeze.

Martha took a deep breath, her chest rising and falling slowly. "Well, George," she said, her voice soft but filled with satisfaction, "we did it."

George, who was staring out at the now-empty town square, smiled. "We sure did, Martha. We really did."

There was a long pause as they both let the weight of those words sink in. What had started as a small, simple idea—a desire to bring a little more happiness to their community—had turned into something neither of them had anticipated. It had grown beyond them, beyond their small gestures, and taken on a life of its own.

"I still remember that first day," George said with a chuckle. "You were convinced we could make people happier with a few random acts of kindness."

Martha grinned. "Well, turns out I wasn't wrong, was I?"

"No, you weren't," George admitted, shaking his head in admiration. "You always knew it wasn't about doing anything big. It was about those small moments. The little things that add up."

They fell silent again, both lost in their thoughts. In many ways, this had been the most important lesson they had learned through their

Joyful Revolution—that happiness wasn't something you could force or manufacture. It wasn't about grand, sweeping gestures. It was about creating space for connection, for moments of joy, however small. And the town, after years of being caught up in the hustle and bustle of modern life, had rediscovered that truth.

George glanced over at Martha, who was looking out at the oak tree, its branches swaying gently in the evening breeze. She looked peaceful, content, and, in his eyes, radiant. "You know," he began thoughtfully, "I think the best part of all this is that we didn't do it alone."

Martha nodded slowly, still gazing ahead. "You're right. The kids, the seniors, everyone in the town... they all became part of it."

She thought back to all the people they had met along the way. The children who had joined in their games, the neighbors who had embraced their ideas, even those who had been skeptical at first but eventually came around. What had started as a small spark between the two of them had grown into something far bigger—something they could have never done on their own.

"It was never really about us, was it?" Martha mused. "We just started it. The town... the people... they made it what it is."

George nodded in agreement. "That's the beauty of it. It's bigger than us now. It belongs to them."

The joy that had once felt like a fleeting experiment had now become a way of life for the people in their community. Neighbors who barely spoke before were now sharing meals, organizing spontaneous picnics, and coming together in ways they hadn't in years. The town had transformed, not because of any one event, but because of the steady, slow trickle of kindness and connection.

Martha leaned back against the bench, looking up at the sky as the first stars began to appear. "It makes you think, doesn't it? About how something so small can have such a big impact."

George followed her gaze, watching as the sky darkened into a deep indigo. "It really does," he replied. "When we started, I thought we'd just be doing a few nice things here and there. I didn't expect it to change everything."

They sat in comfortable silence for a while, each reflecting on the journey they had taken. The town had become a reflection of everything they had hoped for—an interconnected community where joy was woven into the fabric of daily life. It was in the smiles exchanged on the street, the friendly greetings between strangers, and the sense of belonging that had emerged over time.

Eventually, George broke the silence. "Do you think it'll last?" he asked, his voice tinged with a hint of worry. "Now that the festival's over and the excitement has died down, do you think people will keep it going?"

Martha smiled, turning to face him. "Of course, it'll last," she said with certainty. "Because it's not about the festival or the events. It's about the connections people have made. Those aren't going anywhere."

She was right. The festival had been a celebration, yes, but the true success of their Joyful Revolution had been in the quieter moments—the friendships that had formed, the acts of kindness that had become second nature, the way people now looked out for one another. Those changes were permanent, and Martha knew that even in the quiet days that would follow, the seeds of joy they had planted would continue to grow.

As the night deepened, a group of kids ran by, their laughter echoing through the park. George watched them with a smile, remembering how, not too long ago, they had been the ones encouraging the children to play, to laugh, to embrace the joy of simply being together. Now, it seemed, they no longer needed encouragement. The children had taken the lesson to heart.

"They'll be all right," Martha said softly, as if reading George's thoughts. "They know how to find joy now. And that's something no one can take away from them."

George nodded, feeling a deep sense of peace settle over him. For the first time in a long while, he felt truly content—not just with what they had accomplished, but with the knowledge that the future of their town was in good hands.

"We've done good, haven't we?" he said, his voice thick with emotion.

Martha reached over, squeezing his hand gently. "We've done more than good, George. We've made a difference."

They sat like that for a long time, holding hands, watching as the park slowly emptied and the lights from the festival dimmed. The town was quiet now, but it wasn't the same kind of quiet they had known before. This was a peaceful quiet, one filled with the warmth of connection and the promise of tomorrow.

As they finally stood to leave, George turned to look at the bench one last time. It had been the starting point of so much—of their dreams, their plans, and now, their legacy.

"Come on, love," Martha said with a smile, tugging him gently away. "It's time to go home."

George smiled, wrapping his arm around her as they walked. "Home sounds perfect."

As they strolled through the darkened streets, George and Martha couldn't help but feel a deep sense of fulfillment. Their mission, which had once seemed so small, had blossomed into something beyond their wildest dreams. And while they knew that life would continue to bring its challenges, they also knew that they had given their town the greatest gift of all—the knowledge that joy could be found anywhere, in the simplest of moments.

Their Joyful Revolution wasn't over. It had only just begun. And as they walked home, hand in hand, they knew that wherever life took them next, they would always carry with them the lessons they had learned—that happiness was never far away, that connection was the key to it all, and that, in the end, a world of joy was possible, one small moment at a time.

Chapter 18: The Legacy Lives On

The morning air in the town was crisp and fresh, filled with the soft rustling of leaves and the distant sound of children laughing. The streets, once bustling with hurried footsteps and distant gazes, now held a different kind of energy—a quieter, more peaceful rhythm. It was as if the town had learned to slow down, to savor life a little more, and it all traced back to the Joyful Revolution that Martha and George had started.

Martha and George, now a little older but with the same sparkle in their eyes, were seated at their favorite park bench once again. It had become a ritual of sorts—every morning, they'd come to this very spot, coffee in hand, and watch the world they had helped transform.

It had been months since the Happiness Festival, but the effects of their efforts lingered. The town had changed in ways that neither Martha nor George could have imagined. What had once been a place of routine and indifference had blossomed into a community where connection and kindness reigned.

Martha took a sip of her coffee, the warmth of the cup soothing her old, frail hands. "It's funny, isn't it?" she mused aloud, her voice carrying the same quiet wonder it always had. "I never thought a few simple acts of joy would grow into all this."

George smiled, his eyes following a group of children playing tag near the park's edge. "You always had more faith in this than I did," he admitted with a chuckle. "But look at them. Look at how far it's come."

The town had indeed come a long way. What had once been a few flash mobs and picnics had turned into a deeply embedded culture of kindness. It wasn't uncommon to see neighbors stopping to chat on street corners, helping each other with groceries, or gathering for spontaneous potlucks in the park. People smiled more, laughed louder, and the warmth of connection could be felt in every corner.

THE JOYFUL REVOLUTION

One of the most remarkable changes was the way the younger generation had taken up the mantle of joy. Children, who had once been glued to their screens, now played outdoors, organizing games and little events of their own. They'd learned from Martha and George's example that happiness wasn't found in things but in moments shared with others.

Every Saturday, the kids would hold "Joy Days" in the town square, setting up simple games, bringing music, and encouraging others to join in. It was a beautiful sight—young and old coming together, united by nothing more than the desire to enjoy life's simple pleasures.

On one particular Saturday, as Martha and George sat on their bench, they watched as a group of kids ran by, their faces flushed with excitement. They were holding handmade signs that read "Joy Parade Today!" in colorful letters. The children were laughing, the kind of pure, unfiltered joy that only comes from youth.

"Looks like they're having another one of their parades," George said, a hint of pride in his voice.

Martha smiled. "They've taken it to a whole new level, haven't they?"

It wasn't just the children who had embraced the Joyful Revolution. The adults, too, had found ways to keep the spirit of the movement alive. Local businesses, which had once been skeptical of the spontaneous gatherings, now supported the initiative wholeheartedly. Cafes offered free coffee on "Kindness Mondays," where people were encouraged to sit with someone new and share a conversation. The local bakery had even started a "Pay It Forward" system, where customers could buy an extra pastry for someone in need.

The once disconnected, isolated feeling of the town had been replaced by a sense of togetherness. It wasn't just about grand gestures anymore—it was about the small, consistent acts of kindness that had become second nature to the townspeople.

As Martha and George continued to watch the town's joyful activity unfold before them, they reflected on how their small idea had created ripples far beyond what they'd imagined. It wasn't just their town that had been impacted by the Joyful Revolution. Word had spread to nearby communities, and soon, other towns began adopting similar ideas. What had started as a simple desire to reconnect their own neighbors had blossomed into a larger movement that stretched beyond the boundaries of their small town.

George remembered the day they'd received a letter from a neighboring town, thanking them for their inspiration. The letter had come from a woman named Helen, who had heard about the Joyful Revolution and decided to try something similar in her own town. She organized small gatherings, encouraged acts of kindness, and, slowly but surely, her town had begun to change, too.

"I still can't believe how far this has gone," George said, shaking his head in disbelief. "It's like watching a stone drop into a pond and seeing the ripples go on forever."

Martha nodded, her eyes misty with emotion. "It's beautiful, isn't it? To think that all we wanted was to bring a little joy to our town, and now... well, it's become something so much bigger."

They sat in silence for a while, watching as a group of teenagers set up a table in the park, offering free lemonade to anyone who passed by. An elderly couple stopped to chat with the teens, their conversation filled with laughter and warmth. These small, seemingly insignificant moments were the true legacy of the Joyful Revolution.

It wasn't about fame or recognition—it was about the way people treated each other, the way they came together in times of joy and in times of need. Martha and George had always known that the essence of happiness wasn't in grand gestures but in the connections people made along the way.

As the sun began to set, casting a golden glow over the park, a familiar figure approached the bench. It was Lily, the young girl who had been one of the first children to join Martha and George in their early efforts. She was a teenager now, taller and more confident, but she still carried that same spark of joy in her eyes.

"Hi, Martha! Hi, George!" Lily greeted them with a wide smile, her energy as infectious as ever.

"Hello, Lily," Martha replied warmly. "What brings you by?"

Lily grinned, holding up a flyer. "We're planning another Joy Day next weekend, and we wanted to invite you. We're going to have music, games, and a storytelling session—just like old times!"

George chuckled. "You kids are really keeping the spirit alive, aren't you?"

"Of course!" Lily said, her eyes shining with determination. "You two started something amazing, and we're not letting it go. This town is so much better because of you."

Martha and George exchanged a glance, their hearts swelling with pride. They had always hoped that the younger generation would take up the mantle, but seeing it happen before their eyes was something else entirely.

"We're proud of you, Lily," Martha said, her voice soft but filled with emotion. "You and all the other kids—you've made this movement your own."

Lily blushed, but her smile never wavered. "We learned from the best."

As she ran off to join her friends, Martha and George sat back on the bench, watching the sun dip below the horizon. The park was still bustling with activity, but now it felt different—like the town had finally found its rhythm, a rhythm that was slow, intentional, and full of joy.

The sky was painted with hues of pink and orange as the day turned into evening. Martha rested her head on George's shoulder, her heart full. "You know," she said softly, "I think we've done everything we set out to do."

George placed his hand over hers, squeezing it gently. "I think you're right, Martha."

They didn't need to be at the center of the Joyful Revolution anymore. They had sparked the fire, but the town—and the people in it—had carried it forward. Their legacy wasn't about them; it was about the joy they had inspired in others, the connections that had been made, and the way the community had come together to create something beautiful.

As they sat there, watching the next generation continue their work, Martha and George felt a deep sense of peace. The Joyful Revolution would live on, not because of anything they had done, but because the people of the town had embraced the idea that joy was something that could be shared, something that could be cultivated in the simplest of moments.

In the distance, the laughter of children filled the air, blending with the soft hum of conversations and the gentle strumming of a guitar. The park, once a place of solitude, was now a place of connection, of life, and of joy.

And as the stars began to twinkle in the night sky, Martha and George knew that their legacy—one of kindness, connection, and happiness—would live on for generations to come.

The Joyful Revolution: How Two Oldies Plan to Save the World is not just a story of two elderly friends; it's a story about the power of human connection, the beauty in simple acts of kindness, and the unshakable belief that joy is something that can be cultivated and shared.

Martha and George, through their lighthearted antics, unwavering friendship, and infectious optimism, showed us that change doesn't always come from grand gestures or sweeping movements. Sometimes, it comes from small, meaningful actions—an unexpected smile, a shared cup of coffee, or a spontaneous gathering in the town square.

They taught us that joy is not a fleeting emotion, nor is it something we must chase in material things. Instead, it's in the everyday moments we too often overlook: a conversation with a stranger, the laughter of children playing, the warmth of a community coming together.

As the years passed, Martha and George's mission transcended their own lives, becoming something much larger than the two of them. What started as a simple desire to brighten their town became a legacy that rippled through generations, reminding everyone that joy is always within reach. Through their journey, they inspired not just their neighbors but people far and wide, showing that no matter our age, background, or circumstances, we all have the ability to spread happiness.

In a world that often feels disconnected and weighed down by its challenges, *The Joyful Revolution* reminds us that hope is never lost and that the smallest of actions can lead to the most profound change. Martha and George, two "oldies" with a plan, prove that no matter where we are in life, we always have the power to make the world a little brighter—one act of joy at a time.

As you close this book, may their story inspire you to look for those moments of joy in your own life, and perhaps, start a revolution of your own. Whether through kindness, laughter, or love, there is always a way to bring light into the world.

Because, as Martha and George showed us, saving the world doesn't require superhuman strength—just a little heart, a lot of laughter, and a belief that joy is worth spreading.

Dear Reader,

Thank you for taking the time to journey with Martha and George through *The Joyful Revolution: How Two Oldies Plan to Save the World*. It's been an absolute pleasure sharing their story with you, and I hope it brought a smile to your face, a bit of laughter to your heart, and perhaps even inspired you to spread a little joy in your own life.

This story was born from a simple idea—that even the smallest acts of kindness can have a lasting impact. In a world that often feels rushed, complicated, and disconnected, Martha and George remind us that the simplest things can be the most meaningful. From sticky notes with kind messages to spontaneous picnics in the park, their efforts weren't about making grand changes but about reconnecting with the people and the world around them.

I believe that within each of us is the power to create moments of happiness, whether it's in our own lives or in the lives of others. And while Martha and George may have started their revolution in a small town, the spirit of their mission can live on in all of us, no matter where we are. Sometimes, all it takes is a smile, a kind word, or a bit of laughter to brighten someone's day.

As I close the book on their story, I want to leave you with one thought: joy is contagious, and it doesn't take much to spread it. The next time you're out in the world, take a moment to pause, connect, and share a bit of that joy—whether it's with a friend, a neighbor, or even a stranger. You might be surprised by how much of a difference it can make.

Once again, thank you for joining me on this journey. Martha and George's story is, in many ways, all of our stories. Let's continue their revolution, one small act of kindness at a time.

With gratitude and joy,
Anshumala Singh

Don't miss out!

Visit the website below and you can sign up to receive emails whenever Anshumala Singh publishes a new book. There's no charge and no obligation.

https://books2read.com/r/B-A-IYPWB-PICCF

BOOKS 2 READ

Connecting independent readers to independent writers.

Did you love *The Joyful Revolution*? Then you should read *11th Sense - The Final Defence*[1] by Anshumala Singh!

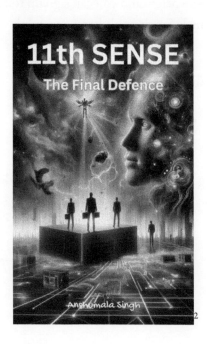

Dear Readers,

Welcome to the thrilling world of "11th Sense - The Final Defence." From the very beginning, this story has been a journey of discovery and imagination—a journey I am excited to share with you.

In this age of rapid technological advancements, where humanity continuously pushes the boundaries of science and the known world, I found myself wondering: What if there were more to human potential than we could ever imagine? We often think of our five basic senses as the limits of our interaction with reality, but what if there were hidden abilities within us—senses we've never fully explored? And what if those senses were the key to saving the world?

---

1. https://books2read.com/u/49R5a8

2. https://books2read.com/u/49R5a8

That question sparked the idea for this novel. 11th Sense - The Final Defence is more than just a thriller; it's a story of unlocking hidden potential and harnessing the full spectrum of human capabilities. It's about a group of individuals, seemingly ordinary at first, who rise to extraordinary challenges. They discover that within them, and within all of us, lie abilities that can change not just our personal worlds but the future of humanity itself.

Thank you for joining me on this adventure. I hope you enjoy the twists, the turns, and the unraveling mysteries as much as I enjoyed bringing them to life. And perhaps, by the end of it, you'll find yourself wondering about your own hidden potential, and what you might do if called upon to defend the world.

Happy reading, Anshumala Singh

Milton Keynes UK
Ingram Content Group UK Ltd.
UKHW040256181024
449757UK00001B/57